DRAGON CHAINS

BECCA BRAYDEN
GRACE GOODWIN

GET A FREE BOOK!

JOIN MY MAILING LIST TO BE THE FIRST TO KNOW OF NEW RELEASES, FREE BOOKS, SPECIAL PRICES AND OTHER AUTHOR GIVEAWAYS.

http://freescifiromance.com

Emily: *i need to talk to you*
  Katy: *i'm working*
  Emily: *it's an emergency*
  Katy: *always is*

"*C*ollins and Rowe, this is Katy speaking. How may I help you?" Katy Toure answered the phone with her most professional voice. She literally cringed every time she had to answer the telephone. Especially right after her boss ran an expensive radio campaign promising free consultations. For each rational human being who called, there were ten crazies and they all thought they had the perfect 'sue them and get rich' case. Katy had more than enough crazy in her life already. She dreaded talking to them and, to be honest, disliked everything about her job.

"Katy! Don't hang up! It's me. Emily."

Katy grinned. Her sister was so dramatic. They may be identical in looks, but that was where the similarities ended. Still, she loved her twin to distraction.

"I'm working," Katy whispered into the phone as she glanced nervously toward the closed door connecting her tiny cubicle to the opulent office currently occupied by her micro-managing boss. "You know I'm not supposed to take personal calls, even when I'm on break. What happened? Is Mom okay?"

"She is feeling better, actually. The nurse said the new lung treatment is starting to work."

"Thank God." Katy felt some of the tension in her shoulders melt. Her mom and her sister were all she had left in the world. Literally. After their house burned to the ground a few weeks ago, she had learned to be grateful they'd all survived. Their stubborn mother had gone back in after their cat, Thorin Oakenshield, Thor for short, and came out with a singed cat, a few minor burns, a broken ankle, and lung damage from the smoke.

Everyone thought their mother had named the fluffy orange tabby after the Avengers character, but her mom was a diehard Lord of The Rings fan. The corner of her mouth twitched up with a quick mental 'thanks' that she and Emily were not Eowyn and Arwen.

Mom had cried more about her burned books and the lost family photos than anything else in the house.

Which was something Katy didn't want to think about right now. They'd lost everything, and her mom had no insurance. None. The whole thing was a disaster with Katy left behind to deal with the mortgage company and bill collectors. Her nerves were just about shot. Emily couldn't help much — she was a nurse who traveled around the world assessing medical delivery systems for her company, flitting from project to project like a honeybee hopping from flower to flower, only to return home every three or four weeks for a few days.

Speaking of foreign locations. "Where are you, Em? I tried to call you last night, and you didn't answer."

"Sorry. Work."

Of course. Emily was always busy helping someone. She put in just as many hours every week as Katy. "So when did you speak to the nurse?"

"About ten minutes ago. She said the new treatment is working. Mom even walked the hall this morning without oxygen."

"Wow. If the lung treatment is working, they'll want to move her to that rehab facility soon. And we can't afford it, Em. Two more bill collectors called last night. I can't believe Mom let her homeowner's insurance lapse."

"That's why I called. I got a contract that will pay for everything, but I need your help. And stop whispering! Who cares if that viper you work for overhears? You're the best paralegal she's ever had, and she totally takes advantage of you. You deserve twice the pay. At least. And if you're at lunch, why are you still answering the phone? You're not even the receptionist!"

Katy had been asking herself the same question lately. "The receptionist quit last month, and every temp we hire leaves within a few days. I'm the only one here."

"You should have quit months ago."

"Someone has to pay the bills around here, especially now." Her eyes darted to the time on her phone. Damn. Her lunch break was over. "I have to go." She hissed, just waiting for the office door to open as it always did at this time. Another reminder that she was under constant observation.

"Wait! Don't hang up. I told you, I landed an amazing contract. I just need a favor to close the deal."

"What kind of favor?" Katy asked suspiciously. Emily tended to start huge projects she couldn't finish alone, then rope Katy in to "help". Most recently it was repairing the wall and repainting their elderly neighbor's bathroom damaged by a water leak. That one day project led to repainting ALL the rooms and a sorely needed deep clean. None of which would have been a problem if Emily hadn't been called out on assignment three days into the project, leaving Katy to finish by herself. She sighed, rubbing her pounding temples. "Whatever it is, I'm not helping this time. I don't even want to know."

Emily's musical laughter filled Katy's ear, setting her teeth on edge. Katy knew that laugh. Hers sounded exactly the same when she was feeling mischievous. She dug her mental heels in. "I mean it, Em. Don't. Want. To. Know."

"You've been saying that since fifth grade," Emily teased her.

"With good reason," Katy countered, stretching her aching muscles. "Besides, I'm exhausted. I've already worked two all-nighters this week trying to get everything ready for an upcoming trial. I don't have the energy for one of your save-the-world projects. Ask someone else this time." She tried to suppress a yawn. Failed. What she didn't tell her sister was that she'd also taken on an extra part-time job waitressing two nights a week just to pay the monthly installment on their mother's hospital bill so they wouldn't kick her out. The medical bills were piling up faster than candy wrappers the day after Halloween.

"I can't ask anyone else. It has to be you. Please?" Emily pleaded, her voice taking on an edge Katy had never heard before. "I'm desperate."

Damn it. Emily had never used that word before. Like ever. Groaning, Katy finally gave in to curiosity. "It has to be me? As in, has to be me because I look exactly like you?"

"Yes."

"I swear, I'm not breaking up with another one of your boyfriends. No more twin swapping. You're just going to have to grow a pair and do it yourself. Come home from Africa or India or wherever you are this time, go knock on the poor guy's door, and say, 'Hi, So-and-So, you're a great guy, but this isn't working for me anymore.'"

"I'm in Alaska. And no. That's not it, I promise. I've been stuck out here in the middle of nowhere for a week, waiting for some engine parts to come in to fix the village's one and only plane. But if I don't show up for the contract job by tomorrow, I'm going to lose it. I already spent the good faith advance they gave me to pay for the first month of Mom's rehab. I just need you to go to Italy, sign the contract for me, and pretend to be me for a few days to make everyone happy. You'll have to hurry, though. My flight leaves in about three hours. Just remember to use my passport since the tickets are in my name."

"*Italy?!* Three hours?!" Katy whisper shouted, her large brown eyes opened wide with incredulity. "Are you kidding me?"

"I'm not kidding. And Katy, this deal will pay me more than enough to cover all of Mom's rehab and pay off the house."

"Is this a joke?"

"No. These people are the real deal and very serious. And rich. Really, really rich."

"Let me guess, you have to pay back the advance if you cancel." Katy sighed. The price of just one month of their mom's rehab would cover the rent on their small, two-bedroom emergency apartment for more than a year.

"I told you, I paid for Mom's rehab. I have to keep this contract."

"What kind of job pays that much?"

"I can't tell you. I signed an NDA."

Perfect. Just like Emily to sign a non-disclosure agreement. "Did you really sign an NDA? Or do you not want to tell me what you're doing because I won't approve?" Nothing new there. Emily had enough wild child in her bones for both of them. Which was why Katy had the steady job and the boring, predictable life. Katy's boss might be a tyrant, but the law firm offered a reliable paycheck.

"It's an emergency. You know I wouldn't ask if I had any other options."

That was debatable. But Emily wasn't a liar. If she said this job would cover all their mom's bills and pay off the mortgage on the burned-to-a-crisp house, she meant it.

"Three hours? Really? That's barely enough time to get to the airport and through security, let alone go home to change and pack! And what kind of papers are you signing that you can't e-sign? Everyone signs papers online now. It's a thing! You can even buy a house that way! Are you buying a house? In *Italy*?"

Emily laughed. "Calm down. Not everyone likes to sign online. There is a property involved as part of a larger negotiation. These people are traditional. Eccentric. They're Italian. Old money. Like ancient castles, old. They insisted on an in-person signature. No big deal. I even had a corporate attorney look all the papers over. These people are legit. As for the trip, you'll be fine. I packed all the essentials when I was at your place a couple weeks ago. I knew I would be on a tight schedule, just not quite this tight. Go home, grab my luggage—it's in the hall closet—and head to the airport. You can eat once you get past security if you're really hungry. When you land, there will be someone waiting to pick you up. Well, waiting to pick me up."

Katy's stomach lurched. "Italy? I don't know, Em."

"My passport and ticket are in the front pocket of my carry-on."

Too bad their passports had been in a fireproof safe in the basement. If they'd burned, Emily wouldn't be able to ask her to go to Italy on such short notice. "I can't leave. What about my job? What about Mom?"

"Your job stinks. You can find a new, better one after you get back. And you have been taking care of everything since the fire. Let me help you out. The doc said she'll be in the new rehab facility for at least six weeks. They'll treat her like a queen. Please say you'll go?" Emily cajoled. "You need a vacation. You can hang out by the pool. Maybe do some shopping. I'll meet you there by the end of the week. I promise. Twin swear."

Katy squeezed her eyes tightly shut, her heart filled with longing at the idea of strolling the streets of Italy, wearing a sundress and sandals, shopping, sipping Italian wine. The vision momentarily buried her misgivings. Was that why Emily had been so secretive lately? She should have pushed her sister harder. Instead, she'd been so busy working extra-long hours trying to cover all the bills, she'd ignored her sister's unhappiness, assuming that, like her, she was stressed and worried about their mother. Tired from working so hard.

Katy groaned. They'd always dreamed of going to Italy together. How did her twin always manage to make everything sound so simple and appealing? "And that's it? Show up, smile, and pretend to be you for a few days?"

"Exactly!" Emily clapped her hands through the phone, her words filled with relief. "As I said, I already reviewed all the paperwork. All you have to do is sign my name. Thanks, Boo!"

"Wait! I haven't said..." Katy cut her words short at the telltale click as the line went dead.

Great. Now all I have to do is tell my boss I need another week off and hope she doesn't fire me. Or pray maybe she does.

2

Caverns beneath the palazzo:

M *ate. Chains. Kill.*
Pain.

Ryker of the Draquonir roared. Thrashed. Fought against the heavy weight of enchanted chains holding his massive and deadly dragon form under lock and key. He'd chosen this prison, locking himself away to protect his people from what he was destined to become. The restraints were the only thing keeping his dragon from smashing his way through the cavernous area below his family's ancient estate and destroying everything around him.

The confinement had not been so unbearable at first. The massive underground caverns were the only place he had found large enough for him to rest comfortably while in dragon form, his luxurious suite on the main floor designed for the human side of him, never the dragon. He had moved many of his treasures into the dungeon in the beginning. Now, a large mahogany desk, the only furniture that remained unscathed by his dragon's rage, caught fire and turned to ash with a blast of his fiery breath. His scales flashed like black diamonds in the firelight. In his fury he cared nothing about destroying one of his favorite treasures. His only thoughts? Primitive. The human within buried deep inside the dragon's agony. Its need.

For *her*. His mate. A female he had been unable to find despite centuries of searching. Without a mate he would lose himself forever in the dragon's torment. Become a monster in truth. A savage killer without remorse or mercy.

He would become the horror human myths and legends had named his kind.

In a world where humans believed dragons and shifters mere myth, every precaution was taken to appear human. They were not human. They were Draquonir; dragon shifters. Magical. Powerful in either form, bound only by the rules the Draquonir race had set for themselves. Only other magical beings were allowed to know of their existence, or true mates of the Draquonir, but even then, only as their true mates breathed their immortal dragonfire.

To share the information any sooner, or with anyone else, would result in a death sentence for them both . Therefore, the caverns, the chains, the existence of shifters, all were kept secret. The gatherings of his people kept underground. Hidden away from those that would fear and attack rather than understand. So many ancestors had been hunted and slaughtered. Discretion was the key to survival for the Draquonir and Ryker held that responsibility above all others.

"Hang on a few more days, my king. All the arrangements have been made." A disembodied masculine voice came through a speaker buried somewhere in the rock, somewhere the dragon would not see. Ryker had invested in a high-tech surveillance system. This was not medieval times, even if the dungeons were far older than even that. His family estate was ancient, but the interior was modern, updated to include every amenity.

Ryker swung his massive head toward the familiar-sounding voice. Struggling to understand the human words through the haze of unwavering pain, he shifted on his clawed feet, craned his long neck, and cursed the chains wrapped around his body, layered over his back and wings. The metal was laced with Elven magic. Not even a dragon could break them, which was why he'd begun wearing them, both as a dragon and as a man, several years ago. Or perhaps a decade had passed. He honestly couldn't remember.

The only way to remove the chains was by shifting back into his human form. As a human, he could make the choice to remove them. That was not an option for

Ryker. Without the chains he would lose control, the form he took would make no difference. Not anymore. Years had passed since he'd been in complete control of his dragon, and the beast was intelligent. Cunning.

Impatient to hunt for a mate.

Now it was too late.

His dragon hissed at the thought, breathing fire at the voice that dared disturb him.

"Ryker? My brother?" That voice again.

Ryker bellowed, his roar shaking the foundation as he struggled in vain to regain control, to shift, his dragon more and more resistant to the change. He was nearly immortal, yet without a mate his dragon would slip over the edge into madness. There would be no last-minute salvation. His time was at an end. He was in pain.

He was ready. Better to die an honorable death than become a merciless killer.

His giant claws scraped the floor, the sound echoing eerily in the empty room.

"Arrangements have been made. Brother, listen to me. She is coming."

Brother? What arrangements? Who is coming? He fought to understand the human words. To remember.

"Ryker," said the voice grimly. "I'm coming in. Don't eat me."

Ryker lowered his massive head toward the small, human-sized door, his dragon's eyes narrowed suspiciously as the thick, Elven metal panel swung open without a sound. The voice seemed familiar, but was the owner of that deep baritone dragon or man?

Memory fragments of a large crimson dragon flashed through Ryker's mind.

Dragon.

Ryker drew back one massive forearm, ready to strike. One of his kind dared challenge the king?

Snarling in fury, Ryker let out a fiery, thunderous warning, his mind full of chaos and confusion.

The door snapped shut just in time to keep Ryker's burst of angry flame from reaching its target, only to open again just as quickly. Before Ryker could inhale again, ready to char the other dragon to cinders, a man stepped through the door.

Ryker reared back. Hesitated. Another memory, this one of childhood, flashed to the fore.

Vector.

Brother.

Grasping for control over his dragon, Ryker held fast to the childhood memory as he stared into the emerald-green eyes of the man before him. Human thoughts emerged. Human memories of them speed shifting. Accidentally setting his younger brother's hair on fire. Ryker had laughed for hours while Vector fumed and plotted revenge.

Slowly the dragon faded, allowing his human side to finally seize control once more. Before shifting he directed one last stream of flame over his brother's head, this time purposely aiming high. A fraction lower and he would fry Vector's hair off again. Ryker laughed, the sound a cross between a snarl and a snort.

Vector stayed where he was, his eyes glowing dangerously. "Still not funny," he growled, his hand combing through short silver curls. "Took a year to grow it back, asshole, and now look at it. I should have red hair. Red. Not this silver crap."

Ryker recognized the mournful tone of his younger brother, a brother not so far away from suffering a fate similar to his own. Madness. Fury. Dragon chains holding him bound to the earth until the executioner arrived.

Sobering at the thought, Ryker finally shifted into human form, using dragon magic to dress himself in leather shoes, pressed black pants, and a white shirt. The massive chains shifted form with him, the Elven magic designed to hide them as nothing more than casual gold chains around the neck of an average man. He looked every bit the billionaire business executive he was in the human world. "You continue to risk your life coming in here. While I am grateful, as your king, I am ordering you to stop. I fear next time I will be too far gone to recognize you."

This time it was Vector who snorted, his suit one Ryker recognized, made by the finest tailors in Rome. "You may have won your place as king, but you are still my brother. I will hold on as long as you do."

"That is what I am afraid of. When my human mind goes, the dragon will have no mercy on whoever walks through that door. I do not want to kill you. You earned your place as second in line. Our people will need you to lead them through the war."

Vector scowled. "No. You will hold on as long as we need you to. A few more days. I will not give you to the executioner's blade, not yet. All the arrangements have been made."

"Ah yes. The arrangements," mused Ryker, ignoring the tingle at the back of his head. His dragon was already pulling at him, trying to take over again. "Has the woman arrived?" The female who would carry his child. Continue his line. The female who had agreed to be mother to his legacy, for a price his clan was desperate enough to pay.

"No. That's what I came to tell you. Ms. Toure has delayed her flight again. She should be arriving late tomorrow."

"Tomorrow." So long when every moment was an eternity. "Very well. Once she signs the documents, you will do what must be done. Notify the executioner. Prepare the Draquonir to mourn their king. Sing the songs of our ancient royal line and prepare for war."

Vector was second in line, but the other clans would not recognize his right to rule without a display of dominance. Power. Vector would have to fight to preserve their clan's territory once Ryker was dead. Their territory. Their dragons. The wealth and lands handed down for generations.

"I am sorry, Brother. I did not wish this for you."

Vector sighed, his emerald eyes ... dragon cannot be bargained with. We all ... truth." He took a deep breath. "Are you sure she ... your mate?"

Ryker grit his teeth. Emily Toure. Long, curly black hair. Sultry brown eyes. There had been a brief moment when he'd thought she was his mate. Even his keen dragon senses had been fooled. One whiff of paradise and then...nothing. His dragon, already unstable, went crazy, spinning wildly out of control with pain and heartache after their initial meeting. He'd finally lost control; the momentary joy, taken from him just as quickly, was catapulting him into an early grave.

"I am certain. Did she say why she needed to postpone this time?"

Vector shook his head. "No, but when I told her if she was not here tomorrow, you would void her initial payment, she promised she would be here." He paused, his eyes straying sadly to what remained of Ryker's desk. "I hope your plan works. If it doesn't..."

Ryker nodded. "I know, Brother. I know. It's too late for me, but if this plan works, you and the others might be able to do the same before it's too late to save what's left of us."

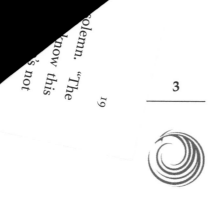

3

Friday afternoon:

Katy walked across the gangway with a sigh of relief, the wash of early summer heat a welcome, soothing embrace after her mad dash home to grab Emily's things, followed by a very long flight. Glancing between the weary travelers walking off the airplane with sloped shoulders and puffy eyes to the small crowd of people waiting just on the other side of the gangway, fresh and eager to board, drove home just how exhausted she really was.

Someone was supposed to meet her here. Or rather, meet Emily. Not knowing what to expect, Katy had taken the time to freshen up before landing with a quick swipe of clear lip gloss and a careful sweep of the mascara she always kept tucked in her small purse.

Thankfully that was all the primping she needed, her skin naturally smooth and clear. Her long hair was another matter altogether. She could already feel stray curls escaping from the artfully sloppy bun she'd arranged on top of her head. Her thick, heavy hair had a mind of its own on good days and a bad attitude on all the others.

With little time to spare trying not to miss her flight, Katy had chosen not to exchange the long navy-blue skirt and cream-colored blouse she'd worn to work. She assumed whomever she was meeting would take her more seriously in her work clothing than in a pair of comfy yoga pants and a T-shirt. Emily had warned her these were serious people. Old money. Castles. Millions, maybe even billions of dollars tucked away in trust funds and investment accounts.

Old-fashioned, she'd said. And that kind of family would not appreciate athletic wear and sandals for a business meeting. Even if she had just gotten off an airplane.

Again a nagging worry crept into her thoughts. Exactly what had Em packed for this trip? They may be physically identical but their idea of fashion didn't always mesh. Emily, when not wearing scrubs, was the epitome of flamboyant styles and bright colors, whereas Katy's closet was a study in sensible, professional blues, beiges and coordinated business suits. The few fun items she did own seemed to always end up in Emily's wardrobe. Katy whispered a plea to no one in particular that at least a few of her things had ended up accompanying her on this adventure.

Surely one of those four gigantic bags I checked in at the airport will be full of shoes? That was the one thing they both agreed on. Shoes make the world a better place and whomever has the most wins.

Glancing down as she smoothed a hand over the wrinkles in her skirt, she nearly collided with a very large man. "Oh! I'm so sorry. Pardon me. Er... *Mi scusi*?"

Where had they come from? How did she not notice them before?

"*Buonasera, Signorina* Toure. We welcome you back to Italy."

Shit. They're here for me? ALL of them?

Katy took a moment to look the group over. Four men, each the size of a tank. Even in expensive suits they looked like spies or military with bulging muscles, short hair, and dark sunglasses. All of them. The two women were nearly as tall and drop-dead gorgeous.

Genetics were so unfair. She's always wanted to be a Mediterranean beauty. And the men...the men were stunning. Powerful. And the one who had spoken to her had shocking silver hair. Through his dark lenses she could see that his eyes were a brilliant shade of emerald. They didn't look real. Was he wearing contacts?

"Is there a problem, *Signorina* Toure? Are you unwell?"

Crap. She was staring. Problem? There was a problem. But she didn't dare say *they* were the problem; they were scary big, brooding, and gorgeous.

She shivered with sudden apprehension.

Not mafia. Please, Emily, not mafia.

Katy took a deep, slow breath and pasted on her best fake smile. *Calm down. Don't overreact. You can do this.*

All she had to do was remember the rules for successful twin swapping. If someone makes a comment or asks a question Emily would understand but Katy did not, she would throw out a fact or two about herself instead. Always speak the truth so she wouldn't have to remember any lies that might trip her up later. Last resort? Distraction.

"*Buonasera, signor.* I am well. Thank you. I mean *grazie.*" Katy forced herself to relax, releasing much of the tension between her shoulders. Emily had said these people were legit, so Katy needed to give them the benefit of the doubt. "I'm afraid my Italian is terrible. Thank you for meeting me at the gate. I hope it wasn't too much trouble getting past security?"

The silver-haired man tucked a placard with Emily's name on it into the inner pocket of his suit, gave a half smile and the tiniest of nods. "Airport security is never a problem. We have an arrangement. I am best known by the name Vector, and these"—he pointed to his companions from left to right—"are the triplets Mist, Frost, and Fury. Blade and Ash are cousins. If you would give your carry-ons and baggage claim ticket to Fury, he and Frost will collect your luggage while the rest of us escort you to the car."

Ash? Fury? Blade? No one has names like that. Obviously not real. Maybe military call signs? Well, maybe Ash and Mist are real names. Ash might be short for Ashley. And Mist, well, that's a pretty name. Frost could be short for Jack Frost. That guy is seriously lacking in the melanin department. But Fury? Blade? No way. They look like they could chew nails for breakfast. Good looks and expensive clothes can't hide that kind of tough. Katy shifted from one foot to the other to relieve the pain in her aching feet.

"Baggage claim. Right." Katy rummaged in her purse for the ticket, handing it over to Fury with an Emily-style grin full of good humor and mischief. "I hate that part of traveling, don't you? If you don't mind, I'll hold on to the one bag. It has all my documents in it." She patted her smallest carry-on containing Emily's passport, tickets, and a few essentials.

Fury scowled, completely unmoved. "Our only priority is your safety. Any luggage kept with you could become a liability in an emergency, putting all of us in danger. Better to give it to me than lose it."

Katy clutched her bag closer to her chest. *An emergency? What kind of emergency, exactly? And why did Emily need so many escorts? Surely one driver with a car should have been enough?*

Confidence rattled, her smile faltered. They all looked dangerous, but Fury looked like the type of man holding back his rage by the thinnest thread.

"Don't mind my brother, *Signorina* Toure," said Mist with a smile as she stepped in front of Fury, jabbing him in the stomach. "He's always like that. I think he's still bitter about being the youngest. Of course you may keep whatever you wish. We are your guardians, not your wardens."

Guardians? What the hell did Emily get herself into? Breathe. In through the nose, out through the mouth. Her heartbeat slowed a fraction as she straightened her shoulders. She was quiet, perhaps, but not a pushover. "My guardians? I assure you, I am in no need of babysitters. I can take care..."

Fury snarled through gritted teeth, "We're not babysitters. We're Guardians. The most lethal..."

"Enough," snapped Vector. "Collect *Signorina* Toure's luggage and bring the car to the back. We'll meet you there once she is processed through customs."

Fury nodded stiffly, turned, and stalked away, followed by a silent Frost.

"*Signorina*, we are running short on time. Please follow me." Vector didn't wait for her response, simply turned on his heel and began walking toward a set of doors she hadn't even noticed before.

Katy had no choice but to follow. Whatever was going on, she had a role to play. Emily wanted her to sign papers, so that's what she was going to do.

Her heels tapped on the tile floor as she made an

effort to keep up with Vector's much longer legs and purposeful strides.

Mist easily kept pace on her left, while Blade took up a position on her right. The other female of the group, Ash, followed silently behind. Katy was surrounded on all four sides. She would bet even the queen of England had never felt so well protected.

The VIP treatment didn't stop with bodyguards and luggage retrieval. Whisked through the door on the side, they walked a short distance to an elevator, down to a private suite complete with a very comfortable looking couch and refreshments.

"*Signorina* Toure," Vector said with a satisfied grin, "a customs agent will arrive shortly to stamp your passport. In the meantime, please make yourself comfortable. This is a private suite. No one will disturb you here."

"Terrific. Thank you." Katy helped herself to a chilled bottle of water, then sat and pulled out her phone. She quickly switched off the airplane mode to send Emily a message. Her fingers flew across the keys as she typed:

*K*aty: *Just landed. What's with bodyguards? Sure about this deal? Not mafia, right? Did you pack my one-piece?*

. . .

*K*aty sipped at her water as she waited for a reply. She longed to take off her stiletto heels and rub her aching feet before curling up on the overstuffed couch but resisted the temptation. She was hoping she wouldn't be here that long. A quick buzz in her hand drew her eyes to the phone.

*E*mily: *Hey. Lots of guards at the estate, too. Don't worry. Pretty sure not mafia. Real estate $$$. No one piece. Sorry. Bikinis all the way. Also did a little shopping.*

*K*aty frowned in confusion as a winky face emoji popped up on her screen. Before she could text a reply, a uniformed customs agent rushed through the door, his face tense. He stamped her passport without more than a glance her way, then left again.

From the suite they sped through the airport on an electric cart, Katy again in the center. Her four 'Guardians' surrounded her, facing outward with Vector driving at a determined, almost dangerous pace.

She was more than a little surprised when he drove the cart out of the terminal. He stopped alongside a super stretch Mercedes limousine; half of her sister's luggage stacked on the luggage cart as Fury loaded the second bag. Wrapped haphazardly around each large bag was black and yellow security tape. If it weren't for the luggage tags, it would be nearly impossible to identify the bags at all. They'd been nearly destroyed. She could see slash marks all up and down the bags exposing clothes, toiletries, and one of her favorite heels.

Damn it, she knew her sister was still 'borrowing' all her best shoes.

"What the hell happened to my bags?" Shocked and horrified, she turned and looked to the right, then left. No one seemed fazed by the dilapidated condition of her bags, least of all Vector.

"Do not worry, *Signorina* Toure. We will protect you," Vector said offhandedly as he stepped out of the cart to address Fury. "Any other problems? I expected you to be here long before us."

Fury scowled. "They inspected every bag by hand. Twice. Slashed through the top rather than break the locks. They all passed inspection, though, so whatever they were looking for wasn't in there. He will need to hear about this."

"Agreed." Vector scanned the area, well aware the 'he' Fury referenced was none other than their king. "Anything else I need to know about?"

"The usual." Fury's lips tightened. "Frost is handling it."

Tucking a stray curl behind her ear, Katy held her

breath and listened with growing concern. Vector had said they would protect her. Protect her from whom? Was she actually in danger? Who were they talking about? An icy finger of fear crept up from her stomach to wrap around her chest. Was Emily in trouble? Was she in danger here? What the hell was she, no, what were *THEY*, now involved in?

Vector nodded grimly. "Very well. Finish loading the bags and let's get out of here."

Katy stepped from the electric cart and walked toward the limousine door Vector opened for her. About to step into the cooling comfort of the air-conditioned vehicle, a loud scraping noise made her pause with one foot inside, her hand balanced on the door.

There on the ground lay her sister's torn up bag, the tape holding the fabric together broken clean through. A dozen or so bra and panty sets lay strewn haphazardly on the ground. Some lacy, some thong, all matching along with a few satin baby-doll nighties and silk camisoles. Katy groaned, her face flaming with embarrassment. She squeezed her eyes shut as she removed her foot from the car, practically running toward the spilled items as her guards bent to help her retrieve them.

"It's okay. It's okay. I've got it," Katy mumbled as she stuffed items back into the bag as quickly as possible. She grabbed the red baby-doll nightie from the ground, realizing too late her sister had used the soft material to wrap something else. A long slender box rolled out, landing atop Vector's foot. There, in big bold letters, were the words "Extreme Turbo Power Bullet with Remote Control."

Katy gasped, frozen in place as one by one their gazes trailed from the bullet back to her. Mortified, face flaming, ears burning, she couldn't get a single word out. Emily had packed a sex toy, and they all thought it was Katy's! She wanted to sink under the ground and stay there for the rest of the week. Finally, without thinking, she squeaked out, "That's...that's not..."

"Yours?" Mist laughed and gave Katy a wink as she picked up the box and casually stuffed it back into Katy's bag. Returning to help Katy with the rest of the clothes, she whispered conspiratorially, "Whoever said diamonds are a girl's best friend didn't have a bullet."

Katy only nodded, still too embarrassed to say anything rational as the limousine was loaded with the rest of her bags. Although it seemed like hours, only a few minutes passed before the entourage was comfortably settled in and the limousine sped out of a small side gate and into traffic. *Dear God, what's next? Can this day get any worse?*

She shouldn't have asked.

After a twisting, turning car ride that made her slightly motion sick, she was escorted into the darkest, most dreadful office she could ever have imagined. The wood was dark. The floor was dark. The walls, the drapes, even the lights seemed dim and only slightly illuminated the room. The chill inside was a stark contrast to the bright, sunny day outside. It reminded her of a cave, minus the dripping water and squeaking bats.

She sat on the oversized leather sofa, trying to be patient as Vector left her alone with Mist. After at least twenty minutes of awkward silence, Vector strode back in the room, his posture indicating a man under extreme stress.

"My apologies. We will not be able to sign the contracts this evening," he informed her, a note of sadness and frustration in his voice.

"Okay. I understand." That was fine with her. All she wanted now was to get out of these shoes, take a quick shower to wake herself up, and maybe enjoy a stroll through the enchanting village she'd seen from the car window as they approached the estate.

"Tomorrow morning? Shall we say ten?"

"Yes, I will be ready at ten." She tried to sound calm and professional but was really thrilled. Ten would mean she could sleep in, take her time. Maybe even wander around this gigantic estate she'd barely caught a glimpse of as she was whisked into a guarded garage and to this gloomy office. "Since you will not be needing me right now, would it be possible for me to freshen up? It was a very long flight and I would like to see if any of my luggage is salvageable."

"Of course!" Vector winced as if she'd shamed him.

"Mist, escort the lady to her chambers and see to it she has everything she needs."

Mist nodded and held out her hand to indicate Katy should precede her out of the room. When they were in the hallway, Mist stepped up beside her.

"This way." She led Katy down a series of stone hallways lined with tapestries and treasures that must have cost a fortune. They walked on rugs that probably cost more than Katy made in a year at the law firm. The deeper into the castle they walked, the more Katy felt trapped, like a prisoner.

"Am I allowed to leave? I'd like to walk around the village a bit. Do a little touristy shopping. Maybe have a glass of wine?" It was still early. She could shower, grab a quick nap, and still have a few hours to spend before she would need to lie in bed and battle her jet lag.

"Or limoncello. You must try it." Mist chuckled. "Of course, you may go exploring. I am honored to be your guide."

"We don't need the entire entourage?"

"Indeed not."

Katy nearly sighed in relief at the thought of getting away from all the intensity and posturing from the men. And the twin swapping. God, she hated lying about who she was. Trying to be her sister all the time was exhausting. Emily owed her. Big-time.

"Just double-checking since there were so many of you at the airport."

Mist's smile grew wider. "We are in our home territory now. No one would dare try to hurt you here."

As opposed to where? The airport? The next town over?

What kind of insanity had Emily dragged her into?

* * *

*D*eep underground, Ryker's entire body shook with suppressed desire. Power. Agony. His dragon raked impatiently at his insides with invisible claws and pulled, grappled with the heavy chains holding him prisoner.

Now. Now. Now.

Unable to respond through the dragon's heavy layers of emotion, Ryker drew the dragon chains tighter about himself. It was the only way to suppress the waves of magic battering him from the inside out.

Be calm, dragon. We will find her.

Something was different about Emily Toure. His dragon sensed it as soon as she entered the main *palazzo*. The beast became crazed. Even now he could barely connect to the dragon's thoughts, fought with every breath to contain him. The creature had never fought so hard.

Mate!

That one word brought Ryker up short. Mate? That was impossible. He'd met Emily Toure months ago.

Touched her skin. Allowed his dragon to take in her scent. She was not their mate.

MATE! The dragon's bellow felt as if it would crack his skull in half from the inside.

Vector entered the room, and the dragon roared a warning.

"Calm down, Brother. She is here. All is well."

But she was not in his home. Not anymore. He'd felt her leave. Known the moment her energy, her presence left the protection of the family compound.

Calling upon a will forged from centuries of struggle, Ryker pushed the dragon deep and regained his human form. "Where is she?"

"My king, she wished to spend some time in the village. Mist and another are acting as her Guardians."

Mine! The dragon clawed at Ryker's insides, demanding freedom to go after her.

His mate.

Dragon flame leaped into his eyes. Ryker felt the burn as Vector stepped back.

"Do not singe the hair off my head. She is perfectly safe."

Ryker's eyes narrowed dangerously as he waved a hand down his clothes, changing them with dragon magic from the suit he'd donned to a more casual look. Black slacks. Blue button-down shirt more appropriate for clubbing or an evening out. The golden chains ever-present around his neck. The Elven magic in the necklace might be the only thing powerful enough to keep him from dragging Emily Toure into the night like a beast and making her his.

His dragon clawed, eager to do exactly that, but Ryker was firmly in control now.

Silence, dragon. We will claim her. Tonight.

Ryker's steel will calmed the dragon as nothing else could. They were in agreement. The female was theirs. Their mate.

Vector stepped forward, looking confused. "What is happening?"

"I am going hunting."

4

Emily: *so how's it going*
  Katy: *fine. sign contract tomorrow. italy is amazing*
  Emily: *told you it would be great. have some fun*

Free from all the problems waiting for her back home, Katy walked along the streets soaking in the sights, sounds, and unique smells of the village in springtime. With Mist accompanying her from the palazzo, she decided to use the other woman as a tour guide of sorts. When she'd asked for a bit of space, Mist had nodded agreeably and followed at a discreet distance.

Katy wasn't crazy or stupid, and knowing she was a female alone in a strange place, she felt much safer knowing Mist was watching over her. She had even asked Mist to let her know if any of the places she wanted to visit were unsafe. Mist readily agreed, even going into the shops with her, then melting into the background. Katy was free to roam, unafraid of getting lost or being pestered by strangers.

The sun had gone down hours ago, but still she didn't want to stop. This was exactly what she needed after the insanity of the last 24 hours. By this time yesterday she had buzzed Bosszilla that she had an emergency and was leaving for a few days then blew out the door without waiting for a response, broken more than a few polite driving rules to get home and then nagged her Uber driver to go faster in her mad dash to the airport. The first-class seat made the flight tolerable, despite her frazzled mental state, but the hours of quiet gave her mind too much time to make up dozens of scenarios and come up with even more questions. The whole airport experience was both bizarre and embarrassing and the uncomfortable drive to the sprawling estate seemed to take hours.

After all of that, postponing the whole 'you have to be there to sign these papers' event that started this crazy train was just about enough to send Katy into a full-blown mental meltdown. Now, however, she was much more relaxed. The past few hours had been perfect. A bit of window shopping. A bit of sightseeing. She actually felt like she was on vacation.

Katy enjoyed every moment exploring, stockpiling memories, taking pictures with her phone, tasting the food from local street vendors. She wanted to experience everything, all at once. She smiled, happy to be in the one place she had always dreamed of visiting.

Catching Mist's eye, she motioned with her head toward a nightclub. Mist would either smile and nod that it was a good place to go, or frown and shake her head no. So far, Mist had only said no twice. Katy was not surprised; the places had even looked a bit sketchy. This one, however, looked very upscale. *Discoteca Reale.* Katy used her phone to look up the translation: Club Royal. *Nice.*

After a nod from Mist, Katy stepped eagerly through the doors of the nightclub, glad she had taken the time to shower and change into one of Emily's little black dresses and a comfortable pair of heels before leaving the palazzo.

The music was upbeat, loud, and the people inside were smiling and dancing. She caught a glimpse of Mist melting into the crowd as she made her way to the ladies' room. Normally she would have felt suffocated, but here in Italy, she was grateful for the other woman's unobtrusive presence.

As she opened the door, cool air and modern decor greeted her, a comfortable looking sofa, coffee table, and magazines in one corner, with plenty of stalls farther in to accommodate the largest of crowds. Katy freshened up, even going so far as to let her long hair down. She was in Italy, after all.

When she finished up, she headed out to find a corner table where she could watch the dance floor without attracting too much attention. She wanted to get a feel for the place before she did anything crazy, like dance in front of a roomful of people who were all so much sexier than she was. Her dancing was pathetic. She looked like a stiff robot every time she tried, while Emily, the wild child had joined the hip-hop dance team. Katy had been drawn to the controlled beauty of ballet. Too many years on pointe made her amazingly graceful, but horribly unprepared for clubbing.

Thinking of Emily, Katy took out her phone and dialed her sister, surprised when she answered on the first ring.

"Hey! You must be psychic. I was just about to call you," Emily chirped happily. "Wow, it's loud. Are you at a club?"

"Yes."

"Fantastic. How did it go? Any problems? Everything go okay? Did you sign the contract yet? Have you seen the pool?"

Katy scrunched up her nose as she listened to her sister's endless questions. Finally she interrupted with a laugh, "Slow down! Let me talk!"

"Sorry," Emily said contritely. "To be honest I was a little nervous about sending you out there in my place. But everything here is on schedule. I should be there in three days."

"I thought it was two? What the hell happened now?" Emily could not do this to her. Not again.

"The most bizarre thing. I made it to Anchorage. Flight was supposed to be a hop over the pole to London. Twelve-hour layover and I would have been there with bells on."

"Em. What. Happened?"

"This amazingly hot pilot comes out of the cockpit and tells the plane we're being diverted to Inverness, as in *Scotland*, because of—well, actually, I'm not sure why. Anyway, there's no flight out of here for a couple days. Something to do with the weather."

"What the hell, Em?" How the hell did her sister always get into these situations?

"Don't get mad. It wasn't my fault this time."

Katy rubbed her temple with her free hand. "It never is."

"Well, it sounds like things are going well in Italy. You're there. You're at a club. Did you wear the little black dress I packed?"

"Yes. But... yeah. Well, about things going well, not so much." Katy paused, thinking about the luggage. And the toy. The humiliation. Thinking about it now made her fidget on her chair. "You owe me big-time. I can't believe you packed a vibrator! That's probably why they postponed the contract signing until tomorrow." She practically shouted to hear herself over the pounding music.

A loud peel of laughter forced Katy to hold the phone away from her ear until the sound faded.

"You think it's funny? Well, your luggage got torn

up and your little toy went rolling out of the bag right in front of the people who picked me up from the airport." Katy's lips twitched with amusement at her sister's indrawn breath.

"Really? Oh, well. I don't care about that silly thing. I threw it in at the last minute."

"As far as I could tell, everything else is fine. I don't know why you bother packing toys like that. You're literally a hot guy magnet. Doesn't matter where you are, they always find you. Me, on the other hand, they treat like a leper."

"Oh Katy, stop being so hard on yourself. We look exactly the same. Guys drool all over you, too, but you don't give them the time of day. I'm not sure you even notice most of them. If you would loosen up a bit. Smile. Flirt. Let the poor guy know you don't think he's a lowly worm you want to squish under your heel..."

Katy scrunched her nose. "I do not come across that bad. I just don't have time to date," she replied defensively.

"Normally I would argue, but I'm done dating. Done with men."

"Sure. I totally believe you." She had heard this from Emily after every bad breakup. The hiatus only lasted until the next drop-dead gorgeous man looked her way.

Katy leaned back into her seat with a grin on her face as Emily spiraled into her sure to be long justification of why this time was different. Katy looked around the club, only half listening to her sister. The crown molding in the room was exquisite; the ceiling etched with some kind of plaster art that made the room feel like a fairy-tale ball should be happening, not a roaring nightclub full of normal people out for a good time. Mythical creatures had been molded into the ceiling. Dragons, mostly. A few fairies. Lots of trees and flowers filling in the spaces. The ceiling alone was worth the trip. Only in Italy would a building this old and beautiful be used as a dance club.

"I'm serious. I've been around the block a few times."

What were they talking about again? Oh yes. Men. "That's an understatement."

"Be nice."

"I was." Katy grinned and watched a couple writhe and move together on the dance floor like they were making love through their clothes. Sexy. Hot. She couldn't take her eyes off them as they started to kiss like they were starving for one another.

No man had ever kissed her like that. Not even close. She sighed, jealousy a little green monster twisting in her gut.

Emily was laughing. "Fair. I've dated a lot of men, and not one of them was worth keeping. I'm done. I've had my fun. I want different things now."

"Like what?"

"It doesn't matter. I'm all set, and I'm determined to be happy about it. But you, dear sister, need to get out there. Take the chance to hook up with an Italian sex god and have an orgasmic vacation."

Katy nearly choked on her dirty martini. "You're terrible."

"When was the last time you let loose and had a one-night stand?"

"Um, wow, let me think about that. NEVER. You know I can barely talk to strangers, so picking up a hot guy and letting him see me naked would be next level."

"Fine. How about sex with a boyfriend? A friend with benefits? Coworker? Anyone at all?"

Katy opened her mouth to reply, but her sister beat her to the punch.

"With a man, not a toy."

"A long time." It was probably over a year now, but who was counting?

She was. Fourteen months. Her va-jay-jay was probably covered in cobwebs.

Emily's voice was sympathetic. "I know you don't sleep around, which is fine. But Katy, you're in Italy! The men are gorgeous. No one knows you. Have a little fun. Have a lot of fun! Just relax and enjoy! You deserve this!"

Katy groaned. "I'll try."

"Listen, I'll be there in a few days. Then the real vacation starts for you, Sis. I want you to find someone sexy. Or maybe two someones, and rock their world. I'll expect a full report after the dust settles," Emily chuckled.

"One is more than enough." Katy sighed. "And I don't know how to rock anything."

"Then just let him rock you on his really big co—"

"Em!"

Emily was still laughing when she ended the call. Katy put her phone away and ordered another drink. So, Emily was in Scotland. Which meant Katy was stuck here.

The kissing couple had shifted position, and the woman now had her back to her partner, his thighs directly behind her backside and his hands on her hips. He was kissing her neck, and she looked blissed out. Content. She obviously trusted the man she was with, and Katy wondered if they knew each other or if this was an Italian thing. Their women seemed so sexy and free. More like Emily than Katy would ever be.

But I'm not Katy Toure tonight, am I? I'm someone else. Katy Toure checked out at the airport back home. Tonight I'm Emily. Fun. Flirtatious. Wild. Free.

What would her twin do in this situation? Exactly what Emily had told Katy to do. Find a sexy Italian man who looked like a god and get naked. Have some fun and a few orgasms. Not be alone in bed.

Again.

"*Buonasera, Mia Regina.* May I join you for a drink?"

The deep voice came from a man standing next to her, and Katy tore her attention from the dancing couple to look up. And up.

Their gazes locked, and Katy forgot to breathe. She

flushed with pleasure. Excitement. The fantasy sex god had arrived as if on cue. And he'd just called her something his—she knew at least that much Italian. Her toes curled. Her nipples hardened into tight, aching pebbles. Desire bolted through her body as the air nearly crackled with sexual tension. Out of all the hot, single Italian women in the club, he'd singled her out. Picked her. A glance to the side showed at least half a dozen women glaring daggers at her. She didn't care.

Katy turned back to sip at her drink, observing him from beneath the sweep of her long lashes. His wavy black hair was short and just a little wild. His lips firm, made to pleasure a woman. His eyes, dark and intense, filled with smoldering heat and promise. He was tall, packed with sinewy muscle she could see outlined through his blue shirt with a hint of gold from a chain around his neck. His shoulders were broad, tapering down to a trim waist, making a perfect triangle that only a man who was seriously fit could pull off. He looked like a lean fighting machine. A large, predatory animal, balanced, focused, ready to strike. She trembled, everything feminine inside her responding to the masculine, dominant alpha waves rolling off him.

"Yes. I mean, sì, *signore*." Katy's voice took on a husky sound she'd never heard before. But then, she'd never been this aroused by just looking at a man either. Sex god might be an understatement. He was gorgeous. Perfect. His smell...

God, his smell.

She took a deep breath and closed her eyes as his cologne—she would have to find out what it was because the scent was the most amazing thing ever— surrounded her and made her body burn. Her breasts grew heavy, and her panties were instantly soaked with her desire.

She wanted more. She wanted to bury her nose in his neck and nibble on his skin. Rub herself all over him. Absorb him. Mark him somehow, as hers.

"I'm going crazy." She whispered the words to herself but didn't open her eyes. Not yet. Not when she could still taste his scent on her tongue and her body was on fire. She needed to gain control of herself. Calm down.

"Such formality... you must call me Ryker. And you are no more crazy than I."

She finally opened her eyes only to find him watching her intently, as if he had noticed her odd behavior. Color swept up her cheeks. She thanked everything holy that the club was dark enough to hide her blush. She was acting like...like...

Em. I'm acting like Em. Wild. Free. But it's okay. That's who I am tonight. Not the controlled, responsible twin. Not the demure, reserved woman who has to think of everyone else first. Tonight I can let loose. Be free. No rules. Nothing but pleasure. Tomorrow I can go back to being the responsible one. Tonight I want for me.

She peeked at him again. His smile went straight to her core, and her thighs clenched.

Ryker slid into the seat next to her and placed his hand, palm up, in the center of the table. A blatant invitation.

Katy didn't want to resist. She needed to touch him. She slid her hand into his and gasped as heat filled her entire body. Raw lust. Desire. It was like she'd fallen into a hot bath, and her mind went blank. All she could think about was kissing him the way the couple on the dance floor had been kissing. Pressing her body to his. Feeling his strong hands grip her hips. Her ass. Melting into his heat. Reveling in his scent as it enveloped her. Welcoming his hard cock pounding into her body over and over...and over.

"Dance with me."

Katy's heart pounded in her chest. The club was loud, the music thumping. She shouldn't have been able to hear his quietly spoken words, but his voice was so deep it carried straight to her ears, vibrated through her body, and set her core to throbbing. His English was perfect, the accent exotic. Sexy. Not quite like the other Italians she'd spoken with while shopping. She couldn't quite place it. Didn't care. "Yes."

Katy allowed Ryker to lead her onto the dance floor. As the music pounded around them, he pulled her in close. She went readily into his arms, her body suddenly pliant, melting into his strength. He growled low, pulling her in even closer. Molding her body to his. He bent his head slowly toward her, allowing her time to resist. She wanted this. Wanted his lips on hers.

Without conscious thought, her gaze grew slumberous; her long, dark lashes swept down to cover her eyes as she waited breathlessly for his kiss. He didn't disappoint her.

His lips were pure fire. Heat flowed through her like nothing she'd ever felt before as he conquered her mouth with his own, his large frame folding around her until she felt like they were the only two people in the world. She'd read novels where one kiss made a woman forget her own name but had never experienced it. Until now.

"Ryker."

"Hmmm?" His response sounded as drunk on desire as she felt. They had melted into one body, one being, and she clung to him without shame or hesitation. She moved with him on the dance floor, the music barely registering. He moved, so she moved. His scent filled her lungs, made her feel like she was a wild thing and somehow he belonged to her now. Was hers to do with as she wished.

Was this pure lust? Pheromones? Chemistry?

Katy couldn't help herself. She wanted more. Her head tilted back, her heavy fall of hair encouraging her to expose the sensitive curve of her neck. Her eyes drifted closed on a wave of pleasure as Ryker bent his head to skim his lips over her beckoning flesh, his warm breath sending tingles up and down her spine. She shivered at his erotic touch.

Ryker pulled her hips closer with one hand pressed

to her lower back, the other diving into her hair, tugging her long curls just enough to let her know he wanted more access. To her neck. Her body. He wanted her to surrender. She gave him what he wanted. What she wanted. With her head back, her chest arched up, her heavy breasts tingling as they smashed into his hardness.

She caught her breath as he caught her body, one muscular thigh diving between hers, his hard muscles rigid against her warm center. She was powerless to resist. Didn't want him to stop. She wanted him deep inside her, didn't care who knew, her normal reserve burned to ash by her desire for him. Part of her screamed this was crazy, the rest of her didn't care.

She opened her mouth to ask him who he was. Where he was from. Something. Anything to break the sexual spell he'd placed her under.

One word. She only managed one word.

"Ryker."

5

Discoteca Reale:

yker groaned at the sweet sound of his name on her lips, his shaft hard and aching, his body adjusting to her every movement, every shuddering gasp as his lips devoured hers. He wanted, needed her. *Mine.*

Mate. Keep. Remove chains. Now.

His dragon's demands rang loud inside his head. Ryker breathed deep. Absorbed his mate's scent. Memorized every detail he could, unsure if the trembling came from his struggle to contain his dragon or from his mate this time. He'd waited centuries for this moment. Given up hope. And yet here she was. Long black hair. Flawless skin. Dark, sultry eyes full of mystery. Passion. *Easy, dragon. She is human. She will not understand if you grab her and fly away with her to some remote island to woo her. I met her once. I could have sworn Emily Toure was not our mate.*

True mate. Show her. Remove chains. Now.

Confusion warred with the white-hot, burning need he'd fought from the instant he'd seen her. He tore his lips from hers, every instinct he had urging him to make her fully his before another could claim her. He could figure out what was going on later, when his mind wasn't clouded with such intense emotions, for one thing was very clear—this woman was his true mate.

There were Draquonir, dragon kind, everywhere. Most came from within his domain. His clan. Ryker looked around the crowded dance floor, zeroing in on the outsiders. He had been away far too long. He, unlike some of the other kings, did not tolerate mixing of the clans. Experience had taught him how treacherous the others could be. His own uncle had mated a dragon from a distant clan, only to be betrayed. She had chosen loyalty to them over the love of her mate, slaughtering innocent dragons in the dark of night. Tonight, however, his only concern, his only thought would be for his mate.

Eyes flashing, he allowed his dragon to push dangerously close to the surface to let out a vocal warning too low for the humans in the club to hear. His message was unmistakable. Leave. The woman in his arms was his. Every male and female Draquonir had become aware their king was inside. There was no hiding who he was, the alpha. His dominance absolute and unmistakable.

Excitement buzzed in the air. The tension was palpable. They knew of his predicament. Knew of his dragon's torment. Knew how truly dangerous he had become without his mate and, consequently, his date with the executioner.

The club began to clear, and he captured her lips a second time, teasing, tugging at her full lower lip until she was breathless with anticipation. When he would have ended the kiss, she did not allow it, instead wrapping her arms around his neck and pressing closer. Opening for him.

Ryker didn't hesitate. He plundered the treasure that was her mouth, his appetite for her erupting into a blazing inferno in his blood. He could never get enough of her. Would never tire of her. His large hands clamped around her hips as he lifted her with ease to sit on the edge of the bar he'd maneuvered them toward.

* * *

*T*he cold metal from the bar top seeped through Katy's dress, drawing her attention from Ryker's kisses to what was going on around her. Everyone was leaving.

"I-I think the club is closing," Katy panted, regret blooming in her chest. Disappointment. "I should go."

Ryker pulled her closer, his only response a low growl of denial.

Katy knew exactly how he felt. She didn't want to stop. Didn't want him to stop. For a moment her natural reserve kicked in. Lifting one hand from the bar top, she tunneled through his thick hair. Tugged. "Ryker."

At last he drew back just enough to look into her eyes. He knew his own would be full of hunger. Need. His breath as ragged as hers, he cocked an eyebrow, his dragon too close to the surface for him to speak. His voice would be a mixture of dragon and man, and he had no idea how she would react. He was in control for now. Barely. He waited for a sign from her to continue. He'd never wanted anything as badly as he wanted her now, but the choice must be hers. Always hers.

Katy squirmed. Tugged at Ryker's hair again. He had to listen to her. She had to make him listen. "Ryker. We have to stop. The club is closing." She scanned the room looking for Mist, her pulse jumping in fear. "Even-even my new friend is gone."

The full meaning of her words was slow to penetrate his lust-filled mind. Ryker froze, although every part of him wanted to continue. Make her his. Here. Now. On the bar. On the floor. The place mattered little. He was rock-hard and needed to be inside her, yet honor forbade him from continuing. With supreme effort he relaxed his hands. Put a fraction of distance between their bodies. He would have to risk speaking in order to explain. "Do not fear me. Mist trusts me, knows I would never hurt you. I care for my own. The discoteca belongs to me. We can do as we wish. If you prefer more comfort, I have a suite above here that I use when I want to stay overnight."

Katy nearly melted into a puddle of goo at Ryker's words. His voice, sexy as sin before, had deepened even further. Like magic, each word pulsed through her body. Her breasts became heavy, her nipples tightened painfully, while her inner core throbbed and wept with desire. Every hair on her body stood on end. Tingled with electricity.

Mist knew Ryker? Knew all along who owned the club? And he had a suite upstairs? Every naughty, bad-girl fantasy she'd ever had flashed through her mind, ramped her up even more. She caught her breath. He could take her up against the bar. The wall. The floor. The bed. He could take her. And take her. And take her. Yes. Yes. Yes. Eyes locked to his, she nodded her consent.

Ryker swept her up in his arms, a driving need to hold her close stealing over him. He had her consent. Dragons mated for life. He was no different as a man. He was primitive. Possessive. He needed her. There would be no turning back. From that moment on he would be dedicated to her happiness, his body an instrument of pleasure. Whatever she needed, he would provide. Hot and slow or hard and fast.

Ryker made a swift decision. The bed. Then the bar. He chuckled.

"What's so funny?"

Ryker looked down at the woman he would cherish forever. The woman who was definitely *not* Emily Toure.

The twin. She had to be the twin sister he'd read about in Emily's background report. Katy. He could throttle both of them for whatever scheme they were up to, but he was too damn grateful. Maybe a good, sound spanking on that delectable ass for this one. Later. Much, much later. If she was into that kind of thing. With a grin, he spoke the truth. "*Mia Regina*, you are lighter than air. I could hold you in my arms forever and never tire."

"Oh hell," she panted, his words a soothing balm and a girl's dream come true all rolled into one. "You're a smooth-talking devil on top of everything else, and I'm falling for it. Have you seen my ass?" she asked, wiggling for good measure.

Ryker laughed from deep in his chest, his heart rejoicing. His spirit lifted. His woman was a spitfire. He paused long enough to give her another drugging kiss, pleased that by the time he drew away, her eyes were once again heavy with promise. Need. Her face flushed with desire.

"Hurry," she whispered.

"Your wish is my command." Ryker took the stairs three at a time, then carried her down the long hallway. The door to his suite opened on silent hinges. He stepped through, then allowed her to slide down his body until her feet touched the ground while the door slid shut behind them. He turned her around and pulled her in close so that her back was to his front, the contact igniting a fire in his blood.

Katy moaned as Ryker's hands explored, teased, stroked her through the dress as his lips traveled up and down her sensitized neck. She felt his cock, long and hard, wedged between their bodies. She placed her hands on his thighs, spread her legs just enough to allow him access, and leaned back into him as he lifted the edge of her dress and dived his hand under her black lace panties. His finger unerringly found her center and drove deep. She was wet. Ready. She let out a cry of pleasure as he set up a hard, fast tempo.

Legs weak, hands trembling, she dug her nails into his thighs. His only response was to work her harder, place his foot to the inside of hers and spread her legs wider. His other hand joined the first beneath her panties, two fingers spreading her feminine lips, the other pressing, playing with her clit just the way she liked it. Her toes curled at the intense pleasure. Lightning raced up her spine. She held her breath. She was so close.

"Let yourself go, regina mia. Fly. I will always catch you."

Katy couldn't hold on. An orgasm ripped through her body. She was engulfed by waves of pleasure. She cried out his name as he pushed her over the edge.

Her legs gave out completely, and true to his word, Ryker caught her. She barely registered the opulent decor as he carried her past the living area, den, and into his private rooms. She saw but didn't care about the huge, modern kitchen, the ultra-plush carpet, the crown molding or large sprawling sofas. Didn't care about the heavy wooden shelving packed with books and mementos. Not even the priceless works of art on the wall or the sparkling chandeliers. It was all a blur. Nothing mattered but him. "Ryker."

Katy gasped in awe as they entered the main bedchamber. Hundreds of tiny candles flickered in the darkened room, focusing her attention. Some cast deep shadows along the wall; some were scattered about the floor, giving a romantic, almost otherworldly feel to the room. "How?"

Ryker's face lit up at her obvious pleasure. "Do you like it?"

"Of course," she gasped, "but—but how?"

"Magic."

Katy laughed. "Magic, or great housekeeping?"

Ryker smiled wolfishly as he placed her in the center of his king-size bed and removed her shoes. "Definitely magic."

"Ah. I see." Katy grinned mischievously, feeling

playful. "Well, how about you magic your way out of that shirt?"

Ryker paused, enthralled by the imp he saw before him. So she liked to play, did she? If only she knew she was baiting a dragon. He smiled slowly, unbuttoned his shirt the human way.

Katy devoured him with her eyes as he revealed ropes of muscle across very broad shoulders. His chest and abs were no less impressive. As quickly as her playful mood arose, it was gone by the time Ryker's large, strong hands undid the last button. She knew those hands now. Knew how good they could make her feel. Knew how strong he was after carrying her so easily. Her face and neck flushed anew as he stood before her bare-chested. Confident. Masterful. An alpha in his prime.

She was far from satisfied. His naked torso did nothing but whet her appetite for more. More pleasure. More Ryker. She swallowed, her mouth suddenly full of cotton.

Katy's breathing hitched up a notch as he climbed onto the bed. She didn't remember him removing his shoes, but they were gone. He was all lithe sinew and muscle as he stalked her like a panther, his eyes locked to hers. She couldn't move. Didn't want to.

He started at her feet. His every kiss shot little electric pings through her body. She writhed with need. Wanted him to hurry, to bury himself deep inside her. Fill the emptiness she hadn't even known was there.

She cried out as he reached her center, his hands making short work of her panties, eliminating the thin barrier between his hot mouth and her most vulnerable nub.

His mouth and tongue worked her into a frenzy. She panted. Moaned. Need pushed her higher and higher until she couldn't lie still. Her hips shifted position, arching up for more. His arm clamped her down, held her still as his tongue penetrated deep. His hand took over where his mouth left off, working her engorged nub. She couldn't take any more. Screamed as she was swamped with waves of heat. Pleasure. This orgasm was even stronger than the last. Ryker's only response was a grunt of male satisfaction before starting the process all over again.

Still, she wanted more. Needed, with every breath in her body, for him to fill her. She grabbed his head, her fingers buried in his hair, and tugged gently. She didn't have to say a word. Somehow he just knew what she wanted. What she needed.

He flipped her over to unzip her dress. The zipper caught. Wouldn't budge. With a growl of frustration, he ripped the fabric in two. She should have been angry that her dress was ruined, but instead she thrilled at his eagerness.

Katy rolled to her back, tugged at his belt. Undid the latch. He needed no other encouragement, got off the bed, and removed his pants. He wore no underwear. Her eyes opened wide as he stood before her, his cock hard and ready, the tip leaking in anticipation. He was huge. Long and thick.

Ryker swept her up and resettled her on his lap as he sat on the edge of the bed, her legs straddling his. With one hand he held her locked to him; the other bunched her hair. Tugged at her long tresses until she gave him access to her neck. Her body. With her head tipped back, her breasts arched. He bent his head, laved first one nipple, then the other, pleased at how sensitive she was. How responsive.

"Please. Please."

Ryker growled, every muscle tense. Ready to pleasure his woman all night. To ready her for their joining. "Please what?"

"Please. Now. I want you now. Inside me," she panted, grinding against him.

Ryker could deny her nothing. Positioning her over his cock, he lowered her, one agonizingly slow inch at a time, until she could take no more. They both groaned.

Katy had never felt so full. He was so big he stretched her to the limit. She ached. Throbbed. Her body quaked in reaction to his invasion.

She clung to his shoulders. Didn't move. Couldn't breathe.

"Easy, *regina mia*," he soothed, his hands at her hips holding her steady. "Easy."

As she relaxed, her desire rekindled. His cock twitched inside her. She couldn't help herself. She moved. He slipped in another inch, and she cried out. "Oh God."

Ryker broke out in a sweat and gritted his teeth to keep from driving his cock the rest of the way in. He had yet to bottom out. He knew how big he was. He hesitated, then sent a tendril of magic into her to ease his way. To help her body accept him. She was human. He doubted she would even notice.

Katy was suddenly swamped with the strongest orgasm of her life. It was sudden. Crashed through her like a tidal wave. She screamed in release, her core milking his cock, taking him deeper. Deeper. Her whole body shook in reaction. Her eyes rolled back. The room spun. She'd never felt such intense pleasure.

"Stay with me," Ryker commanded, shocked by her response to his magic. He grinned. Sent her another jolt and watched her fall apart again. "Damn," he whispered, his chest filled with smug male pride.

Katy's nails dug into his shoulders, her body pulsing with need as he lifted her up and slammed her back down over his hard shaft. Again and again. Up he drove her, demanding orgasm after orgasm. In the bed. The shower. The kitchen table. He was relentless. Tireless. All night long he pleasured her, filled her with his hot seed.

At long last, too tired even for one more round of the most amazing sex of her life, Katy's eyes drifted closed as she snuggled into the crook of Ryker's shoulder.

Confident Katy was asleep, Ryker used his magic to float the sheets back into place. He kissed her gently, his heart full of tenderness for his mate. Love.

He sighed. Sleep would be a long time coming. He had much planning to do if he was to be ready for tomorrow. Whatever Emily Toure and his mate had planned, he needed to be ready. He couldn't lose Katy. In an instant she had become the center of his universe. If she left him, if she refused him, his life would be forfeit.

6

Katy: *took your advice. met someone. OMG i think i'm in love*

Emily: *YES! SPILL THE TEA! I NEED DETAILS!*

*K*aty woke with a smile on her face. She stretched. Winced. Her body protested in places she didn't know could protest. All worth it. She sat up, grabbed the bedsheet, and made a sarong out of the black silk. The aroma of breakfast cooking wafted through the air. The smell was incredible. Her mouth watered. And coffee. Strong coffee.

She couldn't help herself. She let out a tiny squeak and danced a little jig on her tiptoes, not wanting him to hear her. Hottest man on the planet picks me, he's insanely good in bed, and he cooks, too!

Katy grabbed her phone and headed for the bathroom attached to his room. After taking care of basic needs, washing her face and finger combing her hair, she sat on the platform by the jacuzzi tub. She wanted to call Emily and tell her twin everything, but she would have to settle for a quick text.

Pushing the button on her phone, she swiped in her code. There, in big, bold black numbers, the time flashed: 9:15 a.m. Her alarm, which she'd set for seven thirty a.m. the day before, had gone unnoticed. She'd slept right through it and was now running late.

"Oh no!" she gasped, her eyes drawn to where she imagined Ryker was standing in the kitchen. She had to leave, had to go sign the contract for Emily in less than an hour. Had to become Emily. A tear tracked down her face. She hadn't even told Ryker her name. He hadn't asked. What would he think of her? Would he care when she left? This was a one-night stand. She'd known that from the beginning. Still, her heart twisted painfully. She wanted more time with him.

Rushing back into the bedroom, she grabbed her dress, remembering too late that it was torn. Panic set in; her heart thundered. Now what? She couldn't go out there with only a sheet. She spun around, searching for his clothes.

There, on the floor, half hidden by the bed, was the shirt he'd worn the night before. Grabbing it, she put the shirt up to her nose and inhaled. It smelled like him. Her heart tripped. As she put it on, her hands shook. She didn't want to leave like this. Didn't want their time together to be over. Not now. Maybe not ever. But it was too late. She was here for her sister. There was nothing she could do.

The shirt was way too big. She had to cuff the sleeves three times to keep them from dangling past her fingers. The length, however, was perfect. She might even be able to make it look like a dress if she could find a belt. She bent down to look under the bed. Yes! She stretched as far as she could go, strained to reach the long belt that had obviously been kicked under there. Just a bit farther...

"I had hoped we could have breakfast together before you got to the running away part."

Ryker's deep voice startled her. She jerked up, hitting the back of her head on the bed frame. "Ouch! Ouch! Ouch! Oh jeez, I'm sorry! I-I was just..." she stammered. Slowly she backed out from under the bed, careful this time not to bash her head again as she pulled the belt free. "I really am sorry. I would love to stay for breakfast, but I'm actually running late. For a meeting."

Katy blushed as she stood up. Faced Ryker. His eyes flashed with something she couldn't quite name as he looked her over. Something primitive. Possession? Hunger? Her nipples hardened through his shirt.

Ryker stepped closer. Dipped his head and kissed her until her knees buckled and she had to lean on him for support. His hands began to roam. If she didn't back away now, she would never make it to the meeting. She moaned in frustration. He was giving her exactly what she wanted, yet she couldn't take it.

"Stay with me. We can spend the weekend together, get to know one another."

"Ryker," she groaned. "I swear I want to. I swear. But I can't. I have to go to a really important meeting. It's why I came to Italy. I'm really sorry."

"Very well. Then I shall take you to this meeting. Promise when it is over, we will spend the rest of the day together. We can—"

"No!" she interrupted. "I mean, that sounds amazing, but I have to go alone. To the meeting. And I'm not sure how long it will last."

"No breakfast. No staying. No postponing the meeting. What, then, *Mia Regina*, can you promise me?"

Katy stared at Ryker, her heart in her throat. This was torture. She wanted so much to stay. "I don't know. I don't know what I can promise. What do you want?"

He kissed her again. Hugged her close as he wrapped her more deeply in his arms. "I want you to promise that after your meeting today, you will come back here. Get to know me. Give us a chance. You see, I am smitten. I cannot allow you to simply disappear from my life."

Joy lit her face. He was perfect. Absolutely perfect. She squeezed him. "I would love that."

"Then say it. Promise me."

Katy laughed. "Okay! Okay! I promise to come back

here and give us a chance! But you must know, I'm not from Italy. I can't stay here forever."

Ryker grinned, satisfied. "We'll see about that. In the meantime, I believe there is a car outside waiting for you."

* * *

*K*aty dashed to the limo, her face beaming as she jumped into the back seat. "Mist. I'm so glad you're here! Yesterday's meeting was rescheduled for ten o'clock. Do you think we can make it on time? I really need a quick shower and change first."

Grinning, Mist lowered her sunglasses and gave Katy the once-over. "We can make it if we hurry, but you'll have to change fast. As in, set-a-record fast."

Katy leaned back with a laugh. Nothing could ruin this day. Nothing. She was walking on cloud nine. "Got it."

Back at the *palazzo*, Mist helped smuggle her in through the back entrance, distracting the kitchen workers so that Katy could sneak past, her feet bare so she wouldn't make any noise.

Once in her room, she took the quickest shower of her life. There was no time to wash her hair. She threw it into a sloppy bun, grabbed the outfit she'd picked out the day before, and was ready in under ten minutes.

Four-inch sling-back heels and a swipe of gloss and she was ready to take on the world. Or a bunch of stuffy old billionaires, at least. She chuckled softly as she took one last look in the mirror, deciding that Emily really did have a knack for picking out clothes that flattered their body type. Black skirt. Red blouse with a scooped neckline. Her waist looked small, and her breasts showed the barest hint of cleavage. Her ass looked amazing, if she did say so herself. Gold hoops and a delicate gold chain completed the look. Sexy, yet professional. She smiled secretively. Only she knew about the racy red bra and panty set she'd selected. Just in case. For later.

She took out Emily's passport. Time for a little twin swapping. She smiled her best smile. Batted her eyelashes in the mirror. Put a hand on her hip and gave a little wiggle. Somehow, those few changes transformed her from the quiet, reserved Katy into playful Emily. Nodding approval at the transformation, she left the room with two minutes to spare.

Katy walked down the hallway, then took the elevator to the lower level. She didn't have time for stairs, and besides, she was still sore from Ryker's marathon lovemaking. She couldn't complain. She'd loved every minute of it. Was looking forward to more. She'd expected a quick brush-off, yet he'd made her promise to come back. If it hadn't been for this meeting, she would have stayed. Had that breakfast.

Remembering the delicious aromas, her stomach growled, reminding her of the missed meal.

As she approached the large, masculine office she'd waited in the previous day, she smoothed a wrinkle on her skirt. Tucked a stray tendril of hair behind her ear. No matter how many times she pinned the damn thing, it always came loose.

She could hear mumbled voices as she approached. Men speaking in low tones. She knocked gently on the closed door, eager to get the contract signed so that she could think about other things. About Ryker.

Vector swung the door inward and motioned for her to enter. She thanked him with an Emily-style smile and wink, then proceeded confidently into the room. And froze. Her mind refused to acknowledge what she was seeing.

There, standing in the middle of the room, freshly showered and shaved, looking every bit the billionaire, was Ryker. Her heart plummeted.

She met his gaze. Time stood still.

Inside her mind, she screamed. Cried out. Pounded her fists against his hard chest. None of that showed on her face. None of the uncertainty. Pain. Heartbreak. Rage. Had Emily met him before? Should she have known who he was? She had assumed they were strangers. He'd never indicated he knew her. Knew Emily. But then, he hadn't asked her name, either.

What if he was Emily's lover? Slept with her, thinking she was Emily? What if Emily was in love with him?

What had she done?

She turned to Vector. Smiled. She wasn't Katy Toure in that moment. She was Emily. And Emily never lost her cool in front of strangers. Never. "So nice to see you again, Vector."

Vector nodded his head in greeting. "The pleasure is mine, *Signorina* Toure. Please, have a seat at the table. We have everything ready for you."

Katy took a step forward. The carpet was so thick her heel tilted in the dense pile and she stumbled. In the blink of an eye, Ryker was there to steady her, one hand at her lower back, the other under her elbow. Her body reacted to the familiar touch instantly, and her knees nearly buckled. Heat flooded her body, fed her hurt. Her sense of betrayal. He'd lied to her, even if by omission. Taken her body over and over, kissed her this morning, asked her to meet him. She was so confused. Maybe he hadn't exactly betrayed her, but her heart said otherwise.

She jerked her arm away. "Don't touch me."

Vector looked from her to Ryker as if unsure what to do. It annoyed her to no end that Ryker had to give a slight nod before Vector moved toward the waiting paperwork laid out in neat piles on the desk. "This way, *Signorina* Toure. This should take but a few moments. I made the changes *Signor* Draquonir requested. Now that you and he have become intimate, there should be no need for the intimacy clause and the—"

"Wait. What?" What the hell was going on here? Had Ryker manipulated her, or Emily, rather, into bed so that he could change a *contract*? Katy shook with rage.

Ryker took a step closer, ignoring her rigid posture. "Allow me to explain."

Katy shook her head and turned her back on him to face Vector. "Explain what?" The only thing to do now was get out of there as quickly as possible. Hope she hadn't screwed everything up for her sister. She was trapped and had trapped Emily along with her.

Or had she? Perhaps she could bluff her way out of this. Save her sister's deal. "I'm sorry, gentlemen, but the only contract that I am willing to sign is the original. If that doesn't suit you, I'll be on my way."

Ryker turned her around with a snarl. "The original? After last night?"

On the inside she was shaking. However, her face, her body language all told a different story. She reached up to touch Ryker's face for the last time, her finger brushing against his lips as she wiggled just enough to draw his attention to her figure. The swell of her breasts. He wanted to use sex against her? Against Emily? She smiled with all the sass she could muster, and said in her sexiest voice, "That's right, sugar. The original or I walk."

"Never."

"Then we're done here." Katy spun on her heel, ready to leave. She'd blown it. Ruined everything. She walked toward the door, her hand outstretched to grab the handle. She needed to talk to Emily and beg forgiveness. Find out what had happened between her twin sister and Ryker in the past. Find out if he'd slept with Emily, made her squirm and beg and explode in orgasm over and over and...

God. She was a mess. What a disaster.

"Wait," Ryker growled as she twisted the door handle.

Katy stopped but didn't turn around again.

She heard papers being shuffled. She closed her eyes. Waited.

"The original contract is ready for your signature, *Signorina* Toure."

Katy turned around, walked back to the table, and signed. When she looked up, Ryker was gone.

7

Katy: *i need to talk to you. it's an emergency.*

Katy: *answer! please! i totally messed this up. EM!*

Saturday, 1:00 p.m.

Ryker put his phone down on the desk, his heart heavy. He'd just sent out the word to his advisors; they were to cancel all the events they had so carefully planned to introduce his new queen to his kingdom. His clan. All but the annual royal ball, which was a tradition even he could not forgo.

The plan had been simple; since he couldn't find his true mate, he would continue his line using modern technology. Emily Toure had been carefully selected. He and Vector had interviewed hundreds of candidates, but Emily was the only one his dragon had grudgingly agreed to consider. And without his dragon's initial help, a human woman would be unable to carry a Draquonir child in her womb.

Now, he and Emily would marry to make sure she was accepted as his queen, and his children would have a mother. All he had to do was remain in control of his dragon until then, escort Emily to a few official functions. Once she was established as queen, the executioner would provide his unique service and it would all be over. No more Ryker.

Now, everything had changed. He'd met Katy. There was no doubt she was his true mate. Ryker combed a hand through his hair. She was everything to him, had been from the moment he'd seen her in *Discoteca Reale*. She was everything to him, yet to her, he was nothing.

Ryker slammed a fist onto his desktop. The heavy wood splintered into dozens of smaller pieces. A long, particularly slender piece jammed into the fleshy part of his palm. He hissed at the sting and yanked the offending splinter out. Blood dripped from the wound onto his expensive slacks. In dragon form, his skin, his scales were nearly impenetrable. His human form, however, was extremely sensitive, just like a real human. He didn't care about the pain, just turned back to stare out the windows again.

Nothing mattered now. He had finally found his true mate, and she was not interested in him. He gazed out at the ocean from the large wall of windows in his private study. His dragon had finally stopped shouting at him for being all kinds of fool. For once they were in complete agreement. He was a fool. Katy had just made it clear that what they'd shared the previous night meant nothing to her. She'd refused to even read the new contract.

His dragon wanted to show himself to Katy. Ryker couldn't have that. Draquonir law forbade him from saying anything until she was fully committed to him. To tell her now would only result in her death.

A brief knock sounded at the door, followed by Vector and a tall figure dressed in black Elven armor, the color so deep Ryker felt slightly dizzy looking at it, as if he were falling into a black hole. A long black sword, etched with ancient Elven symbols, hovered at the man's back, held in place not by a scabbard, but by magic.

Ryker turned from the window to face his brother and their friend, a Dark Elf prince, now uncaring that the executioner himself had come early. Katy was gone. Nothing mattered now. "Elf."

"Dragon."

Ryker looked at his brother in askance, one brow arched.

Vector grinned and waved his hand at Prince Alrik. "Cheer up, Ryker. I've explained everything, and considering our friendship, and the fact that you may have found your true mate, Prince Alrik has agreed to postpone your execution so long as you remain in control of your dragon. You see, no one wants you to lose your mate or your life. So, the solution is simple, Brother. You must woo your woman the way a human man would woo the woman he wants more than life itself so that Alrik doesn't have to kill you."

"Woo her?" Ryker frowned in confusion. "She is my true mate. She either wants me or she does not. She walked away. Her refusal was clear. I need to tell her the truth. Tell her what I am, and let her decide once she knows everything."

Vector shook his head. "Don't be an ass. She is human, and she feels betrayed. I saw it on her face. Whatever happened between the two of you, she now believes it is all a lie. You must woo her. Trust me on this. You can't break Draquonir law and tell her about us. You would put her life in danger. The law is absolute. It protects *all* Draquonir *and* the other magical races. It can't be broken without consequences, not even by a king.""

"Then how does a human man woo a woman?" Ryker's shoulders straightened. If there was a way to win her back, he would try anything.

"Wooing is simple. I do not know why human men have so much difficulty. Respect her. Listen to her. Pay attention to what she likes, and shower her with gifts. And if she lets you into her bed, make damn sure she never wants you to leave it. Got it?"

"Respect. Pleasure. Gifts. Pay attention." Ryker nodded thoughtfully. "If this is wooing, then you are right. Every Draquonir male puts his mate first. Does all those things."

"Exactly. So, get out there and convince her that you are the only dragon for her."

Ryker gave a half smile, grateful he had Vector on his side. He would make a truly formidable enemy. "I assume you have a plan?"

Vector sniffed. "First, you smell like burnt charcoal. Best get cleaned up. Try wearing one of the Armani suits you have hanging in your closet but never wear. They look sharp."

"My suit looks just fine." Ryker stiffened, waved a hand, and changed his clothing. "See?"

Prince Alrik laughed. "Fine indeed, dragon, if you prefer the uptight, twenty years out-of-date look."

Ryker's lips quirked. "That's rich, coming from an elf wearing tights under that armor."

Ryker's barb was met with deep, booming laughter. "No room for tights, dragon."

Vector raised his hand, signaling for them to stop. "Idiots. You would think we were still schoolchildren. Stop bickering and listen. I sent Mist to convince Ryker's mate she has to be at the helipad in an hour, ready for some shopping in the city."

Ryker began to pace, his mind fully engaged in Vector's plan. "Shopping is easy enough. But what about Emily? I cannot have Katy's twin show up here while I am 'wooing' my mate. They do not know we are aware of the substitution, and I dare not tell them or

Katy might use it as an excuse to run. It is the reason I said nothing last night, and will continue to say nothing until she trusts me enough to tell me the truth on her own. Vector, figure out where Emily is and keep her occupied until further notice."

"Good idea," Vector agreed, nodding thoughtfully. "I believe I know just the Draquonir for the job."

Ryker turned to his old friend, his tone sober. "If my true mate does not accept me after this wooing, I welcome the executioner's blade."

Prince Alrik bowed low. "My blade is yours to command."

8

Katy: *where are you?*
  Katy: *Em, this is serious.*
  Katy: *damn it. answer me!*
  2:00 p.m.

*K*aty stared, her eyes big, round saucers. In the center of the helipad was the most advanced private helicopter she'd ever seen. Black and sleek, the chopper had a large three-blade rotor, and a smaller, partially covered rotor at the tail. Other than the door, she couldn't see any bolts or hinges. The entire body was made from one large piece of metal rather than many smaller pieces that would have to be joined together. The landing gear was retractable like a jet, and the entire top was transparent. Anyone riding inside would have an amazing view.

She was no expert, but if anyone were to ask her, she would have said it belonged in a sci-fi movie.

She didn't need to hear Ryker's deep voice to know he'd come up behind her. His intoxicating scent surrounded her like a warm blanket in a storm before he ever said a word. There was something wild, untamed about it that sent her libido into overdrive. Still, she refused to give in to her body's weakness. Her desire. Instead, she squared her shoulders and proceeded to ignore him. He's Emily's problem now. He lied. Tried to manipulate Emily and the contract. Don't let his sexy voice or his bedroom eyes ever fool you again.

"It's the first of its kind outside of the prototype models we tested last year. Have you ever ridden in a helicopter?" He shoved his hands deep into the pockets of his perfectly tailored slacks.

Finally, she turned to face him. "I was told to be here, so I'm here," she said with a fake smile, torn between pretending to be her carefree sister and still angry with Ryker. Angry with herself. "What now?"

When Ryker didn't respond, she looked back over her shoulder toward the helicopter. She could look at anything but him. She was conflicted and didn't much care if he knew. She'd signed Emily's contract. The original, so she could breathe easy about that part at least, but last night was different. Last night was personal. She bit her lip, racked with guilt.

"There are many things I want, *Mia Regina*. For now, I would like to take you on an outing."

As they stood there, the blades on the helicopter began to rotate. The gentle breeze created by the spinning rotors became a roaring wind. Katy's braid was unrecognizable, loosened hair whipping in the wind. She braced herself against the miniature cyclone created by the rotors, one leg pushed back, her head and upper body bent slightly forward.

She squeezed her eyes shut just as Ryker took her small hand in his much larger one and pulled her into the shelter of his arms. She fit perfectly under one shoulder. Together they ran to the helicopter, the door held open by the pilot.

The interior surprised Katy as much as the exterior. Pure luxury. Four seats, two on each side, with drink consoles in between, made the inside look more like the interior of a limousine than a helicopter. Katy sat gingerly; afraid she would scuff the beautiful, buttery soft white leather.

Before she could buckle, Ryker took the belt, his strong hands grazing her skin as he adjusted the strap. One knuckle brushed the side of her breast. Katy hissed, her body reacting to the accidental touch. His hand froze. She looked into Ryker's face, her eyes captured by his hungry gaze.

Katy's nose flared. *Breathe.* "Are you trying to seduce me again?"

"Would that be such a bad thing?" he murmured huskily. "I won't pretend I don't want you."

Katy wrapped her hand loosely over his wrist and pushed his hand gently away. She had to remember she was supposed to be Emily. She had no idea what their relationship was supposed to be like and had no idea how to proceed. She couldn't betray her sister again. *Remember the twin-swapping rules. Don't say anything about Emily that isn't true.*

"Please, Ryker, I've been working in Alaska for weeks. I know it sounds crazy, especially after last night, but it feels like I just met you. Like we don't really know each other anymore. I just need a little time. In a few days I'm sure I'll be my old self again. Besides, I'm still a little irritated that you tried to change the contract at the last minute. I really hate surprises if I'm not the one orchestrating them."

Ryker nodded, then eased into the seat next to Katy and buckled, He smiled slowly, unaware of how boyish and charming he looked. "You are right, *Mia Regina*. I should not have tried to change the contract without consulting you first. I betrayed your trust, and for that I am very sorry. It is, indeed, like we hardly know each other. I propose we start over. We can treat today as if this is our first date. Take things slowly. You can get to know me. Learn to trust me again. Would that suit you better?"

"I..." She paused, not knowing how to answer. Had he just handed her the perfect solution? "And no sex?"

He laughed, leaned forward in his seat, and said with a wink, "I can resist if you can."

Katy let out the breath she hadn't known she'd been holding. "Then yes, that would suit me just fine."

The pilot finished the preflight check, and they rose into the air. Ryker grinned, his eyes full of male satisfaction.

The helicopter flew low over the water, close to the cliffs. The view was spectacular. She could see miles of coastline. Down below a pod of bottlenose dolphins jumped and frolicked in the blue waves. She covered her mouth with her hand, her eyes glued to the scene. She'd always wanted to see real dolphins. What an unexpected gift.

"I see you have spotted our bottlenose dolphins. They are amazing creatures. If you would like, I will arrange a diving trip from the yacht tomorrow or snorkeling if you prefer."

She turned back to Ryker, her eyes misty. Their eyes met. Held.

Oh dear, what have I just gotten myself into?

9

Katy: *are you dead? WHERE ARE YOU?*
　　Katy: i can't keep doing this.
　　Katy: *EMILY??????*

*V*ersace. *Gucci. Louis Vuitton. Cavalli. Prada.* Katy looked from one label to the next, tried to keep her mouth from hanging open. The boutique screamed wealth. Power. Exclusivity. She never would have come into a place like this. The salespeople would have taken one look at her depart-ment-store clothes and turned her away. Ryker, however, insisted.

The flight from the *palazzo* lasted just over an hour. As soon as they landed, Ryker took her hand in his and hadn't let go, insisting that couples on first dates often held hands. She'd given a token protest, but really, how could she argue with his logic? And now, as a very uptight saleswoman approached, she was suddenly glad he hadn't let go. He must have sensed her agitation because he gave her hand a reassuring squeeze.

The saleswoman glanced at Katy, dismissed her, then turned to Ryker. She looked at the cut and style of his suit, practically drooled, and smiled. "What can I do for you today, *signore*?"

Ryker reached into his pocket and pulled out a business card. He handed it to her casually as he looked around. "I've never been here, but my brother recommended you. You will need to close your boutique. We require privacy."

The woman looked down at the card and gasped. Her hand trembled as she looked up again. "Of course, *Signore* Draquonir." She motioned for another associate to close and lock the doors. "Please, follow me to our private viewing room."

Katy had no choice but to follow the saleswoman into an opulent room with a long runway and one extra-long sofa, glass end tables on both ends, and one large coffee table behind the sofa. The entire room was muted with whites, grays, and tans.

She sat on the far end of the sofa. Ryker could have chosen the opposite end but instead sat right up next to her, his thigh rubbing against hers. He pulled her hand over his leg and started playing with her fingers, testing the strength of her freshly painted nails.

Another saleswoman walked toward them. Katy

leaned into Ryker and whispered in his ear, "What are we doing here?"

Ryker lifted her hand and placed a kiss on her knuckle. "We are shopping."

Choking, she managed to squeak, "This is not how I shop. I can't afford anything in here."

Before Ryker could respond, yet another sales-woman arrived, followed by a train of associates, each holding either food or refreshments, which they placed on the long table, ready to serve them. "*Signore* Draquonir, I am the senior manager here. We are thrilled to have you in our store today. May we offer you a cool beverage, or perhaps a light lunch?"

Ryker turned to Katy. "What would you like, *Mia Regina*?"

Stammering as all eyes centered on her, she said the first thing that came to mind. "Well, I would adore a hot cup of Earl Grey tea, and perhaps a bit of fruit, if they have it?"

"And for you, *signore*?" asked the manager. "What can we do for you today?"

"*Il mia amore* requires a new wardrobe. We would like to see your entire spring collection. Once you complete her fitting she will make her selections."

Katy coughed. Choked on her tea. Her hand trembled as she set the cup on the table. *Mia amore*? Did he just call her his love?

"Of course, *signore*. Accessories as well?"

Ryker smiled. "Everything."

The manager put her hand to her throat, her eyes sparkling. "Excellent. And your price point?"

"We have no limit. Call my assistant. The number is on the card I gave your associate. He will set up the account."

The manager nodded and turned to Katy for the first time. "Please, *signorina*, take your time. When you have finished, follow *Signorina* Abbiati to the fitting rooms," she said, her hands twisting. "We have many wonderful items for you to select from. This may take several hours."

Katy jumped up, her heart pounding a mile a minute. She could do this. She could pretend to be Emily and get her twin some amazing clothes. They were exactly the same size. So what if it felt like this was all about her? She just needed to keep reminding herself that this wasn't about her. It was about Emily... Emily, Emily. Emily. "I'm ready."

Following *Signorina* Abbiati to another room, she quickly undressed down to her bra and panties. She was measured and remeasured. Everything got measured, even the length of her instep, the size of her fingers, wrists, arms.

Two of the ladies had been whispering nonstop since they'd come in. Every once in a while she would catch the word Draquonir. Were they talking about Ryker?

Finally Katy could take no more. "I'm right here, ladies."

"*Scusi, signorina,* we do not mean to be so rude. It is that we have many famous people come here, but the Draquonir are most notable. Our manager will get a big promotion if you are happy with us today."

Katy frowned. "Really? Why?"

Signorina Abbiati dropped the measuring tape and walked over to a small table on the side, returning with two magazines. On the cover of both were Ryker and his brother, Vector.

Katy took the magazines and stared. "I'm sorry. I can't read Italian. Can you translate this for me please?"

"Si, *signorina.* It says, 'Italy's Most Eligible Bachelors' on this one, and the other is a business article about the Draquonir empire. They are Italy's oldest and richest family. They have billions, and have recently announced plans to expand into new markets. Whatever they do, others follow."

Katy blushed. "Oh. I see."

Signorina Abbiati shook her head. "No. No. I do not think you understand. You see, *Signore* Draquonir has many female admirers, but he has never taken a serious interest in one until you, *signorina.* We are very excited for you. And for us."

"For you?"

"Si, *signorina.* Your connection to the head of the Draquonir family will generate much interest in our boutique. Your choices here today will influence spring and summer trends in all of Italy."

"Oh my God." Her legs gave out, and she sank to the floor. "I can't do this."

"Oh no!" *Signorina* Abbiati cried out to her assistant, "Go! Get *Signore* Draquonir. Quickly!"

"There is no need," Ryker snapped, pushing the door open and scooping Katy protectively into his arms. "I am already here."

Katy smiled weakly and wrapped her arm around his broad shoulders, oddly glad to see him. "I'm fine. Really. Just a momentary shock was all. You can put me down."

Instead of putting her down, as she requested, Ryker turned to the others. "Leave us."

Katy didn't watch them leave, mesmerized by Ryker's commanding presence. His eyes flashed with something elemental. Possessive. He was in alpha mode, and her body reacted instinctively, her mind a deep pool of need. Her nipples hardened, and her body buzzed with electricity.

There was no avoiding it. She still had nothing on but panties and bra. She couldn't hide her reaction any more than he could hide his. He kissed her. Hard.

By the time he let her up for air, she was breathless and dizzy. He set her down only to walk her back toward the wall. He wrapped his hands around the backs of her thighs and lifted her up, wrapping her legs around his waist. His hard shaft pressed against her, straining through his suit.

With one hand he reached down and ripped

through her panties like they were cotton candy, his need fueling her own. She let out a cry as he unzipped his pants, and with one hard stroke, he filled her. Out of nowhere an orgasm ripped through her. She screamed his name, but he just filled her again and again, pushed through her orgasm and demanded more. Took her against the wall, on the floor. Her voice grew hoarse from screaming his name, which only served to make him redouble his efforts.

His voice, unnaturally deep and guttural, finally penetrated the fog. "Mine."

When they were spent, he dressed, wrapped her in a blanket she hadn't noticed was in the room, and walked with her securely in his arms out the door. She buried her head in his shoulder, too embarrassed to look at anyone as he carried her to the door.

"*Signore* Draquonir, you have not made your selections."

Ryker looked down at his mate and shrugged. "Send one of everything, in every color."

The manager gasped. "One of everything we have? Accessories as well?"

Ryker adjusted Katy in his arms and turned back to the door. On his way out he confirmed, "Everything. You will know what she likes when she wears it."

10

Katy: *you better get here soon. please answer me*

Katy: *this is a nightmare, i'm so sorry. please don't hate me.*

*R*yker's Yacht:
Katy fastened the halter top of her red dress, her cheeks sun-kissed and glowing. They'd spent the whole day on Ryker's yacht, diving and playing with the dolphins. She'd had such a wonderful time, only the setting of the sun and growling in her stomach could make her come in.

Ryker had stayed by her side the whole day, ignoring phone calls and rearranging his schedule. He'd been considerate and asked her questions about her childhood, listening intently to the answers. Trying to be Emily was becoming harder and harder. She found herself slipping time and again, coaxed into relaxing her guard by Ryker's charm and good humor.

Ryker came up behind her, tugged playfully on the ends of her hair. "Ready for dinner? I believe the chef has made something special for us tonight."

Katy turned toward him, placed one hand on his chest. They'd made love several more times, and the guilt was crushing her, but she couldn't resist him. Her heart ached. Emily should be arriving the next evening. This was her last night with Ryker. She needed to tell him the truth. Needed to talk to Emily. "Dinner sounds lovely."

Placing her arm in his, she allowed him to escort her to the elegant formal dining area. Candles and soft music greeted them. Ryker seated her at the end of the table, then joined her. The chef immediately came out, along with several uniformed servers. All day long, whatever she'd wanted, they had been right there, waiting on her. She felt like a princess.

"If the *signorina* is ready, we will start with the first course."

She nodded. The smells wafting from the covered platters were mouthwatering. She had a good appetite and made no apologies for it. They shared a bottle of hundred-year-old wine. When Katy protested, Ryker just laughed and filled her glass again. Course after course was served. Sweet and spicy hors d'oeuvres followed by succulent fruits, tender meats, and the freshest vegetables. Dessert was just as amazing, with a freshly made cup of gelato.

At last she could eat no more. Drink no more. The day had been absolutely magical.

"*Mia Regina*, I have something for you."

"No, no more." She laughed softly. "Please don't ask me to eat another bite."

Ryker took out a small ring box and opened the lid.

Inside was a huge black diamond ring. Katy swallowed. "What is this?"

"This belonged to my mother years ago. It has been handed down for many years. I would like you to accept it." He slipped the diamond onto her ring finger as a dozen strangers came out with rows upon rows of wedding bands.

"What's happening, Ryker?"

"Over these past few days, I have discovered that I want you to have this ring, this symbol of the Draquonir line. You have captured my heart. It would mean a great deal to me if you were to wear my family ring." He waved at the jewelers standing in front of them. "Please, you must select a setting. Choose one that speaks to you."

Katy looked at the settings, her eyes drawn to a stunning piece that would offset the large black diamond beautifully. Unable to resist, she reached out with a trembling hand and traced the line of sparkling white diamonds with a fingertip. A tear leaked down her face. She couldn't do this. Could not choose a ring that would be worn by her sister.

She knew which setting Emily would like, a bold, contemporary piece that was sophisticated and geometric in design. Katy preferred the more traditional setting, the design reminded her of a priceless antique, something that a lady would have worn in centuries past. Holding in a sigh, she lifted her hand from the setting and folded both hands neatly behind her back to make sure she did not give in to temptation again. "I-I'm sorry. I can't do this right now. You must excuse me."

Katy didn't wait for an answer. She left the dining room and ran the whole way back to the luxurious room she'd been given.

She soaked her pillow with tears. Life was so unfair. She was a horrible person. She'd fallen in love with her sister's fiancé. He was irresistible. Sexy. Perfect.

When Ryker knocked quietly, she did not respond. The door opened on silent hinges and he came in. She turned away to hide her tear-streaked face, refusing to look at him. "I'm sorry, Ryker. The rings were beautiful. I guess I'm just tired."

He crawled onto the bed and pulled her body backward, into the curve of his heat. His arm came to rest around her waist and he kissed the back of her head. "I understand, *Mia Regina*. Trust me. Everything will be well. At the party, I will introduce you to everyone as my future wife, but the wedding will not be held until you are ready. I give you my word. Nothing matters to me but your happiness."

Katy sobbed at his words. How was it possible to fall even more in love with a man she already knew she could not keep? She should know better. Resist him.

His heat soaked into her body, addictive as any drug. The soothing strength of him at her back made her feel cherished, adored, protected. The tenderness of his lips in her hair made her want things she should not want.

She wanted to roll over, kiss him and let him make her forget the rest of the world existed. She wanted to tell him the truth. She wanted him to say the things he was saying to her, to Katy, and mean them. She wanted all those things, even though it meant betraying her sister.

The party he spoke of was a ball. Emily had entered it into her schedule as 'Royal Ball', so that's how the event came up on Katy's calendar. So, she had to be Emily for one more night. Pretend to be his queen, his fiancée, his love, while in reality she was an imposter, lying to them all.

How had she gotten herself into this?

Emily. That's how. And right there, soaking up the warmth and tenderness of the man who could never be hers, Katy made a vow to herself. Never again. Never. Life or death, emergencies be damned, she was never going to pretend to be her twin sister ever, ever, EVER again.

It hurt too damn much.

He held her for the rest of the night. Near dawn, emotionally exhausted, she drifted into an uneasy asleep.

11

Katy: *this isn't funny anymore. i'm worried. are you ok?*

Katy: *omg please answer me so i know you aren't dead, ok?*

*K*aty looked at herself in the full-length mirror and did not recognize the woman staring back at her. She looked like a fairy-tale princess.

Or villain.

Either way, she was stunning, and Katy never saw herself as stunning.

The long black dress Ryker had sent to her hugged every curve as if it had been custom-made. The shimmering material was something she did not recognize, but the soft black gown clung to her like silk, glittered like diamond dust. The dress hugged her shoulders and arms, dipping to a sexy valley between her breasts. Not so much that she was afraid she would fall out of the dress, but definitely enough to feel like a goddess. Ryker had even sent shoes to match with heels just high enough to complement the dress, but not so high she would be cursing his name within the hour.

The servants he'd sent to help her get ready were lovely women who apparently did not speak a word of English. They poked and prodded and helped her into the gown. They'd applied her makeup with a professional touch and styled her hair in a corona atop her head that she never would have dared on her own. They'd left several minutes earlier, and now she didn't know what to do with herself.

A soft knock startled her, and she turned at the sound.

"Come in."

Ryker stepped into her room, and her heart skipped a beat. His black suit hugged every muscle, the black shirt beneath made of the same material as her gown. All she could manage was to do was stare. And blush.

And want.

Damn him and damn Emily and damn this whole mess. I've fallen in love with him and one hundred percent betrayed my sister. I'm a worm. A villain in a fancy dress.

Her heart didn't care.

"*Mia Regina*, I have brought you a gift."

Mia Regina. My queen. She'd looked the phrase up after that first night and now wished she hadn't. She wanted to be his queen. Wanted to keep him for herself. "But I didn't—"

"Hush." He placed a warm finger over her lips, and it took every ounce of self-control not to suck his finger into her mouth and start something. "These were my mother's, her mother's before her. For generations." He opened a velvet box he'd been carrying under his arm.

Katy gasped. "But—" Oh...wow. There had to be a genuine fortune in diamonds and gemstones in the box. They were too much. "They're too expensive, Ryker. What if I lose an earring?"

He chuckled as if that were funny. "It would please me to see you wear them tonight."

"I'm not kidding. What if the chain breaks on the necklace? I can't. I just can't."

Ryker lifted a stunning black diamond pendant from the box and walked behind her. He lifted the necklace over her head from behind, and she shivered as the cool metal settled between the valley of her breasts. The huge, rare black diamond, shaped like a teardrop, was surrounded with at least two dozen sparkling, flawless white diamonds. He leaned forward and kissed her bare shoulder as he fastened it in place. "You are mine, *Mia Regina*, and you will allow me to honor you tonight."

He nibbled on the side of her neck as he wrapped

his arms around her from behind and pulled her close. His gaze locked onto hers in the mirror. Held.

With a groan, she finally closed her eyes and leaned into him, tilted her head to give him better access. *Tomorrow this dream will be over. Emily will be here. I'll have to give him up. I'll have to confess everything and hope she can salvage something from the mess I've made. Hope she can forgive me.*

Because tonight? God. Tonight, I want to be his queen. I want him to look at me like he is now, always, like I'm the most beautiful woman in the world. Like I'm the only woman who exists. Like he loves me.

Ryker pulled her in closer. Whispered nonsense into her ear. Nibbled on her neck. Her heart both melted and shattered in turns.

Tomorrow. Tomorrow she would confess the truth to him and watch his gaze turn to hate. But not yet. Not. Yet. She opened her eyes to stare once more at the image of them together in the mirror and could not look away. This was her fantasy come to life, staring back at her from the smooth glass. "All right. If it means that much to you, how can I refuse?"

"Excellent." He kissed her shoulder one more time before returning to the box and lifting a pair of matching black and white diamond teardrop earrings. As she fastened them in place, he brought her the ring. The setting she'd refused to choose but had desperately wanted was there, perfectly highlighting the large center stone.

"How did you...?" Her voice trailed off as he slid the ring onto her finger. Of course, it fit perfectly.

"I pay attention."

She stared at the ring as tears gathered in her eyes. This wasn't right. This ring was Emily's. He belonged to her sister, not her.

Not. Katy.

Emily. Emily. Emily.

If she told Ryker the truth now, he would hate them both. Emily and Katy had both lied to him. Tried to trick him. He would demand Emily pay back the advance, and their mother would be kicked out of rehab.

Katy squared her shoulders. So be it. She would work three jobs if she had to. She couldn't keep up the charade. Things were too intimate. Too personal. Too much falling in love and not enough pragmatic distance from her sister's business partner.

"I don't deserve this, Ryker. You don't understand. I have to tell you—"

"Hush." He placed his finger over her lips again. "Not now. Do you hear that?"

She listened closely and realized music was drifting through the hallway outside her room. Beautiful, haunting music. And the soft rumble of many voices.

"Our guests have arrived. The party has begun. Nothing would please me more than having you on my arm. Please, *Mia Regina*. Give me this night."

She loved him. Heart and soul. Head to toe. Every cell in her body ached to give him anything he wanted. "Yes."

His smile could have melted an iceberg. He turned from her and snapped the lid closed on the velvet box before she could make out the final piece that lay inside. She wanted to know what was in the box, what he hadn't given her. But she was beyond spoiled already and didn't dare ask. She was already playing the villain; no need to make things worse.

He held out his arm, and she wrapped her hand around his elbow, allowing him to escort her from her bedroom toward the party. Vector stood just outside her room.

Ryker handed the black box to him. "When the time is right."

"Of course."

Vector walked away without a backward glance, leaving Ryker and Katy alone in the hallway. The music was louder now, clearly a waltz, and it sounded as if Ryker had an entire orchestra inside.

"Are you ready?" he asked.

"Not even close."

Her honest response made him throw back his head and laugh. The sound made her entire body tingle with longing. She wanted to hear that sound again. A thousand times.

"You are very intelligent. I have enemies here

tonight. Stay close to me. Do not go anywhere without one of the Guardians. Do you understand?"

"No. What enemies? And why invite them to a party?"

All levity gone, he turned her in his arms and lifted one hand to caress her cheek. "I do not fear my enemies. I only fear losing you. I will explain later. Just know you mean everything to me. Everything. Do you understand?"

"Yes." She understood all too well, for she felt the same way. She just could not lie to the man she was falling in love with for another minute. Her eyes burned at the thought of losing him. Of hurting him. Leaving him behind and going back home. Never seeing him again. But she couldn't do this anymore. She would find a way to make things right with her mother. "Ryker, I have to tell you—"

His lips crushed hers before she could complete the sentence, his kiss stealing her breath. Her will. Her very soul from her body. When he finally released her, they were both fighting for control. "You promised me tonight."

"Yes." For one night she wanted to be his queen, the gorgeous, mysterious woman by his side. She wanted him to look at her like he'd never get enough. A few more hours would change nothing. The truth was coming for both of them. If he wanted the dream to go on for one more night, she would play along. She could deny him nothing. Didn't want to deny either of them this last night together. "Yes. I promise. Tonight, I am yours."

He kissed her once more, softly this time, then turned them toward the din coming from the grand entrance of the *palazzo*. When they reached the top of the long, winding staircase, Ryker stopped and surveyed the room, Katy with him.

Hundreds of people mingled below. Beautiful ball gowns, dazzling jewelry, and women so stunningly beautiful Katy was sure they had all walked straight off a fashion runway. They were tall, the women lithe and elegant, the men shockingly handsome in designer suits and shoes that looked like fine Italian leather. No one in the room looked a day older than Ryker or herself. And not one person in the room looked less than royal. Katy had never seen such a thing in her life, not even in the movies.

Ryker placed his hand at the small of her back and led her, slowly, carefully down the winding stairway, his touch a burning brand at her back.

With every step, the room quieted more as head after head turned in their direction. By the time they reached the first landing, even the orchestra stopped playing and literally every eye in the room was on her.

Not Ryker. Her.

Her hand clenched, unseen in the crook of Ryker's elbow. Her throat tightened. Was she having a wardrobe malfunction? Had she grown horns? What was with these people? Was she so far below Ryker's class that they would not accept her among them? No, not her. Emily. Emily. Emily.

Ryker stopped at the landing and walked with her toward the railing, the edge waist-high, and stared down over the throng of guests like a king addressing his court.

"Thank you all for coming this evening. I know many of you are curious about the beautiful woman by my side. I assure you, you will have a chance to meet her after the ceremony. For now..." He lifted his hand toward the orchestra at the far end of the courtyard. "Play something slow. I wish to dance with *Mia Regina*."

Multiple gasps reached Katy's ears before the music grew in volume to overtake them. Ryker ignored them all and turned to look at her. "Dance with me?"

Just as he had the first night, he held out his hand. She slipped her fingers into his hand and allowed him to lead her to the dance floor, her smile as shaky as her knees.

This time they danced alone, the other guests leaving the dance floor empty as they stared.

"Why are they staring at us?"

"Not us, you. Your beauty dazzles them all."

She felt a blush warm her cheeks, but she was no fool. The women here were gorgeous. Every single one of them. She found herself extremely grateful for the stunning gown and jewelry Ryker had provided. Without them, she would feel naked in this crowd. Even with the glittering gown and priceless jewels, many women here were much more beautiful than she.

Still, who was she to argue with the man of her dreams? Especially when he was looking at her like he wanted to devour her.

"You're crazy, you know that?"

Ryker threw back his head and laughed again, the sound causing a ripple of shocked looks to pass from person to person in the room.

"I take it you don't laugh much."

Ryker looked away from her to glance at the crowd. Less than a second later, his gaze was once more focused on her. Their gazes locked, and she could not look away from the pain she saw in his eyes. "I have not laughed in years."

"Why not?"

"Because I had not found you."

Katy gasped as pain, sharp and deep, stabbed her heart. She had to tell him the truth. Bracing herself, she took a slow breath. Perhaps if she asked him to go back up to her room for a moment, she could find the courage to tell him.

"Ryker."

"The rest of the world can wait. You are mine tonight, remember?" he whispered. "You promised."

Katy shuddered. Nodded. Ryker was right. She would give them this happy night. *I bet this is what Cinderella felt like when she went to the royal ball.*

She went knowing it was just for one night, too. I can do the same for my very own prince.

With a grin, he swung her around, twirled her until her head spun, and she collapsed against his chest, trusting him to catch her.

After the first song, more couples joined them on the dance floor, but Katy was oblivious to them all. Ryker's gaze rarely left her face, and the warmth in her body spread with every step, every moment she belonged to him.

"It's time, Brother." Vector's hand appeared from nowhere to rest on Ryker's shoulder.

"Of course." Ryker slowed his steps and lifted a gentle hand to her cheek. "Are you ready to formally meet our guests, *Mia Regina*?"

She wanted to stay in his arms and dance all night, but she knew he was important to these people. Why, she wasn't sure, but he was rich. Maybe even nobility of some kind? She had no idea, but she would stand next to him, smile and shake hands. She could do that. "Lead the way."

Ryker placed her hand in his and led her toward the stage where the orchestra played. There was an open space between the violins and the front edge of the raised platform that had been erected for the event.

Ryker led her to the center, Vector on their heels carrying the black velvet box. From either side, the group that had picked her up from the airport fanned out and stood at attention. They'd been intimidating at the airport. Tonight, dressed to kill in suits and gowns, they looked like deadly assassins straight out of a movie...too pretty to be real.

Ryker held her hand gently as he raised the opposite above his head. Immediately, the room fell silent.

"My people, I am Ryker of the Draquonir."

A low rumbling noise came from the crowd, and Katy would have sworn the temperature in the courtyard jumped ten degrees. But that had to be nerves. Right? What was going on here? Why was she standing in front of a crowd of people with Ryker at her side and Guardians lined up around them like ancient warriors ready to kill to protect them?

Worried, she looked at Mist for a hint about what was happening. Mist caught her look, winked, and grinned back at her.

Katy did feel better, but not much as Ryker continued.

"Tonight I introduce *Mia Regina* and place the sacred Dragon Eye upon her head."

Vector stepped forward and knelt before her. Lifting the black velvet box toward Katy's waist, he held it steady as Ryker opened the box to reveal a crown. A real freaking crown that Katy realized perfectly matched the rest of the jewelry she was already wearing. In the center of the crown was a gigantic black diamond surrounded by sparkling white. The pattern repeated in a full circle with the black diamonds decreasing in size from front to back.

The crown sparkled like it had stars inside each gem. Or fire. She'd never seen anything more beautiful.

"Ryker. I—"

He paused, crown in both hands, his gaze lifting to meet hers. "You promised me tonight."

"I know, but—"

He leaned forward and kissed her in front of everyone. When he ended the kiss, the crown was on her head, clinging there as if by magic. She'd felt nothing. No pins, no poking or prodding. In fact, the thing felt light as air.

The crowd erupted with a sound she'd never heard before. Not clapping or shouting.

Are they roaring? Mia Regina. Mia Regina. *Dear God. They think I'm going to be their...their what? Their queen?!*

Frantic, about to be sick with her new level of betrayal, she grabbed Ryker by the hand and dragged him off the side of the stage and into a side corridor. Once they were alone, she lifted the crown from her head and placed it in his hands. "Ryker, I can't. I can't accept this. You don't understand."

With a grin she now found more infuriating than adorable, he lifted the crown back to her head and then cupped her face in his palms, gently, his thumbs stroking her cheeks, as if she might break. Which wasn't far off the mark. She was about to shatter into a thousand tiny pieces.

"Tell me then. Why can you not be my queen?"

Katy closed her eyes. "Stop touching me. I can't think when you touch me."

"Then I shall never stop." He chuckled but let her go. "My attention is yours. Tell me what bothers you."

She closed her eyes and sucked in air, hoping courage would come with it. "I'm not Emily Toure. I'm Katy Toure, her twin sister. I've been lying to you the entire time."

12

Royal Ball:

*R*yker could not bear to see his mate in tears and lifted a hand to gently wipe her cheek. "I know exactly who you are, Katy. I have known from the moment we met."

Katy stilled, certain she'd misheard. "What did you just say?"

Ryker tensed. The sorrow he'd seen in her eyes flashed to anger faster than a lightning strike. "I know you came here pretending to be Emily. I have always known. We belong together. There is no one for me but you. Of course I knew. I could never mistake you for another. Not even an identical twin."

Katy shook with suppressed rage. Hurt. "I've been

worried this entire time, feeling like the very worst person on the planet, and you knew?"

The fire in her eyes made him ache to shove her against the wall, lift her dress, and take her here. Now. His cock swelled with eagerness. Unfortunately the Draquonir had excellent hearing and her cries of pleasure were for no one's ears but his own. "I waited for you to trust me enough to tell me."

"I don't trust you!" she yelled, her heart broken. Aching.

"Do you not?" His dragon raged at her denial, clawing to break free and prove himself worthy of their female.

"No. Well, if I did, I don't anymore. You lied to me!"

Moving slowly, giving her every chance to escape him, he stepped forward, slowly backed her against the wall. When she had nowhere else to go, he lowered his head until his lips hovered over hers, the lightest of touches, his breath synced to hers. "You do not run from me, even now. You come apart in my arms. You gave me your body and your heart. You are mine, Katy, and I will not give you up."

Lips tingling, Katy's shoulders loosened just a little. She wanted to sink into him. Wanted to trust him. Wanted to believe they could be together forever. She was so confused. "What about Emily? And your contract?"

"Null and void."

She moaned. "I've ruined everything then."

"You saved me, Katy. Gave our people hope. How is this a bad thing?"

"My mom. You don't understand." She turned her head to the side, breaking the contact between them.

He took advantage by lowering his lips to her bare shoulder. The side of her neck. Seeing her in his colors, the black gown sparkling around her like black fire, the royal jewels wrapped around her throat brought him more pleasure than he'd ever imagined. He'd expected to find a mate and make his claim. Have children. Continue the family line.

He had not expected to be obsessed with every expression and sound she made. To crave her presence like a drug. To need her touch, her happiness more than he needed his own.

He had not expected to fall in love.

A single tear full of pent-up emotion, of heartache, tracked down her cheek. "Ryker. Stop. I can't. I can't do this. It will ruin everything."

"Tell me," he whispered soothingly as he wrapped his arms protectively around her, grateful she didn't resist the comfort he offered. He needed to comfort her. Protect her. He did not understand why she was so upset, had expected her to be happy that she didn't have to pretend anymore. Had they really expected to fool him? Fool his people? He had completed extensive background checks on Katy and Emily both. He knew where they worked. How they lived. He did not see a problem.

"My mother needs this really expensive rehab facility, and we used the money you gave Emily to pay for half of it. If the deal doesn't go through, my mom will be kicked out, and I can't take care of her in my little apartment. Emily is always gone, flying here and there, and I never know when she's going to be around to help. And my boss is a serious bitch—I mean, she's horrible. I'm already working two jobs, and I just can't do this. You have to take Emily back."

Ryker wanted to throw back his head and laugh at his mate's groundless fears, but he didn't dare. She did not trust him. Not yet. Had no idea the lengths he would go to ensure her happiness. She was clearly upset and very worried about her family. One more reason he had fallen for her. She would make an excellent queen for his people. For him. And she would learn what it meant to be his. To be cared for and protected.

Rocking her gently in his arms, he held her until she relaxed against him, her cheek pressed above his heart. "You are mine, Katy. My mate. My queen. You do not need to worry about such things. I am wealthy beyond what you could possibly imagine. And what I have, *Mia Regina*, is yours. I would never leave you to deal with such troubles on your own. I will take care of you and your family. Do you understand?"

"No." She pulled back to look up at him but did not resist his embrace. Thank all that was holy, because he could not let her go when she so clearly needed him. "I don't understand this at all. You've only known me for a few days. And now I'm in this dress, and I have a crown on my head, which makes no sense at all. And you keep calling me your queen, but queen of what? I'm not the queen of anything. And why would you even want to take care of me? My life is a mess. My job stinks. My mom is sick, and the medical bills are crazy. My sister lied to you. I lied to you..."

Her voice trailed off as he lowered his head to kiss her forehead. Her temple. The side of her face. Her jaw. "I have not been completely honest with you, either, my love."

She stiffened. "What does that mean? You're married, aren't you? Or engaged?"

"No. Nothing so simple."

Katy swallowed nervously. "Worse than you're already married?"

"No. Yes. There are many things I must tell you. But first, I need you to know that marrying me will mean so much more than living in this *palazzo*. I want your full commitment. Here. Now. Tonight."

Ryker kissed her, only Draquonir law keeping him from baring his soul and admitting that he was not entirely human. That she would be revered and respected by Draquonir all over the world, and hunted by others.

That when he made her fully his, the black dragon-fire would engulf them both and change her body chemistry. Magically tie her life force to his. Make her more than human.

Desire burned through him as she sighed, her hands exploring beneath his suit jacket, fingers tugging at his body as if she would never get enough.

"My king!" Vector slid into the hallway, the words a shout on his lips. "There is trouble. You must come at once."

Slowly, with a reverence he knew he would feel with no other, he lifted his head, never breaking eye contact with his mate. "Stay here? Wait for me? We have much to discuss."

She nodded, her gaze darting to Vector.

Ryker straightened, his attention zeroing in on Vector. Only something truly serious would faze him. Vector was clearly enraged, his hands clenched into fists, dragon magic lit the back of his eyes.

Mist and Fury appeared behind him, grim expressions on both of their faces.

"Who has dared disturb us this night?" Ryker had made it known to all the Draquonir, his clan and all the others spread across the continents, that he had found his mate and would present her to his people tonight. He had invited the elder elves and high-ranking members of his allied Draquonir clans. Only a rival would be foolish enough to cause trouble on such a sacred night.

Or someone who wished to start a war.

"They wear no clan colors," Mist offered.

"Drifters, then." The Drifters were those without loyalty or allegiance. Exiles and troublemakers. Thieves and mercenaries. And very, very dangerous.

Facing Katy, he lowered his forehead and pressed it to hers. Their gazes locked. "I am in love with you, Katy Toure. Not your sister. You. Please, stay here and wait for me while I deal with this."

He nearly lost control when she placed a small hand on his cheek, leaned in, and whispered into his ear. "Go, then. I'll be here when you get back. And I'll expect you to tell me everything."

Turning his head, he placed a kiss in the center of her palm and tore himself away from her. He hated leaving her behind. Hated walking away from her. His dragon screamed in rage, cried out for blood, demanded justice for the Drifters who dared threaten their mate.

"You two, do not leave her side. Protect your queen with your lives. Understand?"

"Of course." Mist and Fury spoke in unison.

Satisfied that Katy would be protected, Ryker followed Vector to the tallest rooftop on the estate, and they shifted, one black dragon and one red, surveying the chaos below as his people, some in dragon form, some still appearing human, engaged with the Drifters and protected their queen.

His roar was answered by his clan, and he took to the air, eager to be done with this and return to his mate.

* * *

*K*aty was sure her sigh could be heard through the entire *palazzo*. She turned to Mist, whom she knew and trusted. Fury was fine, no doubt, or Ryker would not have left him behind. But Katy didn't know him that well, whereas Mist was familiar. A friend. "What is a Drifter? And what is he talking about? I don't understand any of this."

Mist tilted her head to the side, her look sympathetic, but gave nothing away. "He will explain everything to you later, Katy. Why don't we get you somewhere more secure than this hallway?"

Fury scowled. "Too late. Someone comes."

Mist crouched into a fighting stance. Balanced. Ready. "Friend?"

"No." Fury's face turned grim. "We cannot shift here."

"No. We cannot."

He sighed and pulled two daggers from leather sheaths strapped to his back, well concealed beneath his dinner jacket. "The hard way then."

Mist reached between her breasts and pulled out a bodice dagger with a two-and-a-half-inch blade of heat-purpled steel, the leather sheath sewn into the bodice for concealment. Bending down, she used one of the blades to cut off most of her skirt as Fury watched with a grin.

"Not one word, Fury."

"I didn't say anything." He did glance down at her shoes. "You're leaving the heels on?"

Mist smiled and the expression would have frightened Katy if she didn't know the other woman was on her side.

As one, they turned to face the far end of the hallway, clearly hearing something Katy could not.

"Get behind me and stay there," Mist ordered.

Katy wasn't going to argue. She had no idea what was going on and was still trying to process the fact that Ryker knew who she was. All this time, he knew, and Katy wasn't sure whether she should be relieved or furious with him for stringing her along. But she'd been lying to him, too. If he knew, why didn't he speak to her earlier? Why not confront her with the truth? What was he trying to achieve? Surely seducing the twin sister of the woman he'd already agreed to marry hadn't been part of his plan.

Before she could put any kind of logical thought process together, four strangers sauntered around the corner, walked confidently and with purpose toward them.

"You are not welcome here." Fury did not yell or seem to be surprised. He didn't raise his voice at all. Did he know these people?

The tallest one, clearly the leader of the group, responded with a grin. "An oversight, I'm sure. Your king would not introduce the first contract breeder without inviting the other clans."

Contract breeder? What the hell was that supposed to mean? Katy stiffened. She knew an insult when she heard one.

Mist actually growled, the sound making Katy tense. And maybe just a little scared. "You're an ass, Erik. Take your Guardians and get out."

The man in the center had hair so blond it appeared white. His suit looked expensive, and he was far too handsome. But then, so were the three men surrounding him. They looked like Nordic myths, fairies or elves or something she might see in a fantasy movie. No one had that coloring in real life. Compared to Mist and Fury's dark hair and eyes, they looked like aliens.

Erik, the leader, ignored both Mist and Fury and looked straight at Katy. "Ms. Toure, I presume."

Mist swung her blades in a threatening arc. "Do not come any closer."

Erik tsked at her. "That won't be necessary." He looked back over his shoulder. "Gentlemen?"

The two closest to Erik stepped forward and raised what looked like a cross between a harpoon and a crossbow, took aim, and fired. A net of floating silver shot from each of their weapons to cover and entangle Katy's two protectors.

Mist screamed in pure feminine rage, not pain. Katy knew the difference. Mist wasn't hurt, but she was really, really angry. Spitting mad. "How dare you use Elven magic against us! That is an act of war."

Erik placed a hand on top of one of the crossbow-style weapons and pushed it down. The other man lowered his weapon as well, and Katy realized she'd been holding her breath in anticipation of being shot as well. Adrenaline raced through her system.

"Ms. Toure, you are in no danger from me. I give you my word."

"Don't listen to him. He's an ass," Fury ground out between frustrated struggles against the net holding him prisoner. The netting was so fine it looked like spiderwebs covered with fresh dew. It should have been easy for either Mist or Fury to break.

Both struggled. Katy lifted her head to the men who stood before her, her eyes wide. "What do you want?"

"Simply to speak with you. You will not be harmed."

Katy looked at Fury, who growled, to Mist, who glared at Erik but clearly spoke to her. "Don't be afraid. Ryker will kill him if he touches you."

Erik chuckled at Mist's words. "He is welcome to try." He turned his gaze from Mist back to Katy. "However, that will not be necessary. Ms. Toure, please, I assure you, I simply need to discuss your recent bargain. You will not be harmed."

He looked at Mist and raised a brow as if chastising a small child. "And this would not have been necessary had your king been reasonable regarding my request to meet the lady."

"She is no concern of yours." Fury pressed so hard against the net Katy could see blood welling up on his cheeks in a pattern that matched the net's. The fine thread was literally cutting through his flesh.

Katy tried not to show them how much she was afraid and hid her trembling hands behind her back, her shoulders straight. With both Mist and Fury out of commission, she didn't have much choice. She was no match for four huge blond men, each at least a head taller than she and probably twice her weight. She could try to run, but she hadn't taken running seriously since middle school when she would run from boys shoving worms in her face.

"You won't hurt them?" she asked.

"Mist and Fury will remain unharmed. Please." Erik held out his hand, and Katy stepped forward but kept her hands behind her.

"I am perfectly capable of walking. Don't touch me," she said in her most regal, you-can't-scare-me voice, walking sedately as if she were out for a casual stroll around the gardens. She may not be a real queen, but she could pretend for a few minutes.

"As you wish. Follow me please." Erik turned on his heel and walked back the way they had come. Behind her, Mist shouted Erik's name as Fury bellowed in rage. The three Guardians with Erik fell in around her like a circle of protection. Erik walked for a few minutes then turned and walked down a stone stairway to what felt like private tunnels or underground passages. Katy had no idea as she had never explored this part of Ryker's estate.

She'd been too busy in Ryker's bed to look around.

Erik paused before a heavy wooden door and turned to face her. "If you would please remove the crown, my dear, we shall leave that behind. The pendant as well. There are rules even I will not break."

Katy had completely forgotten she was still wearing a fortune in diamonds. She lifted the sparkling crown from her head and looked around for a place to put it.

"Anywhere will do." Erik pointed to the floor.

Seemed a shame, but...

Katy set the crown on the floor, followed by the necklace, and stood to face Erik. "Now what?" She covered the ring she wore with her opposite hand. That she could not bear to remove.

"Now we shall go somewhere we can have a nice, sensible discussion."

One of Erik's Guardians opened the door and led the way outside. Each lifted their weapons as they moved together across one of the smaller courtyards, with Erik and her in the center of the circle.

Thunder rumbled in the sky, and Katy looked up, expecting to see clouds. A storm. It was early evening, but dusk had not yet given way to night. She shivered with apprehension.

The sky was clear. Beautiful. She could hear the crashing of the sea far below the cliff the estate rested upon.

Erik and the others led her to a door in the estate's tall stone wall. "Where are we going? We can talk here."

Erik laughed. "Oh, no. Not here. Ryker is too hot-headed at the moment to see reason."

Obviously arguing would do her no good, so Katy followed as Erik led her through the gate, her arms crossed protectively in front of her.

The cliff edge was no more than thirty paces away, then dropped off to the Mediterranean Sea far below. The smell of salt and seaweed, fish and sand surrounded her. The rhythmic sound of crashing surf and thunder made the hair on the back of her neck stand on end.

Then she heard a roar. Not that of a lion. Nothing so small. This sound came from the sky itself, loud as the thunder from twenty simultaneous strikes of lightning.

She jumped. Looked up. And up.

What the...?

Two large beasts crashed together in midair, their bodies twisting and turning around one another as they plummeted toward the water. One black, one red. The black creature released the other and soared back into the sky as the red creature careened out of control toward the water.

Katy blinked. Eagles? Seabirds of some kind? Huge, gigantic scary seabirds?

What was that?

"I see Ryker has not told you everything."

Tearing her gaze from the strange sight, Katy looked at Erik. "What do you mean? What are you talking about?"

"He has not told you what we are."

Erik watched the same spectacle as she, except he did not look confused. He was smiling.

Another roar grabbed her attention, and she whirled back to face the open water just as the red creature erupted from the water. It climbed toward the black as the black—God help her, she was going to say it—dragon plummeted from high in the sky in what looked like an attack dive. Fire, or what looked like fire, came from the black dragon's mouth.

"Oh my God." Her hands closed over her mouth in shock. Disbelief. Fascination.

One of the men behind her chuckled. "God isn't going to help you."

"Silence." Erik chastised the man, but it was too late. Katy's heart, already pounding with adrenaline and fear, beat double time.

The black dragon attacked the red once more, biting, clawing, tearing at the red dragon's wings, locked in a deadly battle.

"My lord, you'd better send Talon up there. Ryker is in a killing rage."

Erik nodded, his gaze never losing sight of the two dragons. "Yes, I see that."

Katy gasped. Surely they weren't implying Ryker,

her Ryker, could be one of those dragons up there? She looked up again, her fear growing exponentially as she watched the red dragon slash at the black dragon's underbelly.

She turned to look at Erik, who was watching her with a speculative look in his cold blue eyes. They were like ice, a glacier frozen behind each eyelid. "Go."

One of the three Guardians took off at a run, and Katy lost sight of him.

"The car is this way, Ms. Toure. If you'll follow me." It wasn't a question nor a request; it was an order, and they both knew it.

In a matter of seconds their small group walked under cover of overhanging rocks and spindly trees that clung to life on the side of the cliff, the thin roots a chaos of twisting white lines just above her head. The ledge they walked on was not wide, yet her shoulder repeatedly brushed the rocks as one of the Guardians kept pace, walking between her and the steep drop on the opposite side.

The roaring faded the farther they walked, and in a few minutes Erik led her to a small clearing where a long black limousine awaited their arrival, another blond giant opening the door for them as they approached.

"After you." Erik stepped aside and waved his arm, acting the gentleman, as he waited for her to climb into the vehicle. Adjusting her gown, she stepped inside the most luxurious car she'd ever been in. Erik followed her inside, sat beside her. She scooted as far away as she could get from him.

Erik sighed.

She glared. She'd just been kidnapped, and he had the nerve to act like she was the one being unreasonable.

Seconds later the car was in motion.

Totally faking a bravado she didn't really feel, she tapped her foot impatiently and demanded, "Where are you taking me?"

"Somewhere you'll be safe."

"Why?"

"Many lives depend on the answers to my questions, Ms. Toure."

Katy crossed her arms defensively. "I don't know anything."

"We shall see."

13

Dragon:

diot human! Remove chains!

Dragon threw himself against the sand, his tail thrashing wildly. A large, stray boulder that had fallen from the cliffs years earlier burst into pieces with one swipe of his tail. The dried remains of a tree limb splintered in half, broke, and were driven deep into the sand. With a monstrous roar he tried to throw off the chains holding him prisoner, focused his magic in an attempt to melt the offensive Elven metal for the thousandth time.

Nothing. His human had been silent since the two dragon opponents had turned tail and run away. Dragon was too weak to give chase. Bleeding. Torn. His wings badly damaged. He needed half a day to heal.

Too long! His mate was gone. Taken.

Dragon seethed. *Ryker! Remove chains! We go. Destroy enemy.*

No! Ryker argued, the human voice inside the dragon's mind. *We don't know where Erik took her. Let me out.*

Hunt! Now! You failed. Human Ryker had his chance to protect our mate. To claim her. Dragon will make things right. Find mate. Destroy enemies. Give true mate my dragonfire.

Every swipe of his tail caused ripples in the sand like raindrops in a shallow pool of water. Around him, the rocks and sand took on a reddish hue as dragon blood soaked the earth. Eventually he would break free. He was ancient. The oldest of all living dragons. He would not be defeated.

"Ryker!" Someone farther up the beach yelled his human's name. Who dared approach? Dragon waited until the fool drew near and blasted the intruder with fire. A fellow dragon would be immune to the flame. An ignorant human would burn.

Dragon was out of patience.

Rather than turn to ash, as Dragon expected, the intruder continued to advance on his position, enveloped by a silvery glow.

Dragon sniffed. Elven magic.

Dark elf.

Dragon roared in fury.

"Ancient One," said the dark-haired man covered

in black Elven armor. "You called for the executioner. I am here."

Dragon turned his head. Raged. Swung his massive body to face the elf. Bits of sand, rock, and salt water flew from Dragon's tail to douse the elf, but the ancient magic woven through the elf's armor held steady, and the assault melted away, not harming the elf at all.

A low rumble was the only warning Dragon would give. If Dragon could not burn the elf, he would crush him under talon and claw. Tear the elf to pieces. Break free of these chains.

Hunt. Go to his mate.

"Dragon! Do not force me to kill you today. We were friends once. Do you not remember?"

Dragon swung his head back and forth, fighting the memories that accompanied the all too familiar voice. Dragon had great magic inside him. Magic so ancient, so wrapped in mystique and legend, few could comprehend the extent of his power. He narrowed his gaze. Lowered his head to stare at the one sent to kill him.

I remember you, Prince Alrik. Dark Elf scum. You dare threaten me? You cannot kill me. I am a dragon.

"Old friend. Do not make me do this. Calm yourself. Allow me to speak to Ryker."

Dragon snarled. Roared. Breathed fire at the Dark Elf, but the bastard stood his ground, hand on his sword hilt, completely unaffected.

Asshole.

That finally had an effect. Prince Alrik threw back his head and laughed.

Tired from the battle and from berating the human inside him, tired of trying to break free of the dragon chains, Dragon gave one last heaving breath of fire and allowed Ryker to regain control over his form, gave in to the change.

* * *

*E*xhausted and bleeding, Ryker pulled himself slowly to his feet, his only thoughts of Katy. He had ruined everything. He never should have allowed the invaders to breach his defenses. Should have tripled his guard. Not been so arrogant. Should have listened to his dragon and told Katy the truth, revealed his true nature, Draquonir laws be damned, and bound her to both parts of him. Once she was fully his, he would have found a way to keep her by his side.

Coward. His dragon scolded.

"I know, Dragon. Silence. I've had enough." Ryker had acted out of a need to protect his mate from the Draquonir laws, but also out of fear. He admitted to himself that he had been terrified of losing her when she discovered the truth; he was centuries old, an ancient dragon shifter. A creature of myth and legend. A monster in disguise.

Now she was gone.

He shook his head and stumbled forward, blood dripping with the steady beat of a leaking faucet into the sand.

"They ripped you to pieces." Vector had arrived on the beach and now stood next to the dark elf, Prince Alrik.

"You are fortunate they did not kill you." Alrik's tone held no jest, merely a statement of fact.

"It wasn't me they were after." Ryker's voice was dry and rough from battle and breathing fire. "I welcome your presence, Alrik. I need only your skill with that blade in battle, not as my executioner. My true mate has been taken from me."

Alrik nodded solemnly. "Your brother has informed me of your mate's abduction. If she is your true mate, you must fight for your sanity. Your dragon has become too powerful. You know this. Remain in control of him and lead the hunt to find her. I will honor my vow to your kind if necessary, but your death would be a great loss to all Draquonir. And"—he scowled—"I believe Vector has located King Erik's private jet."

* * *

Katy sat in her cushioned leather seat aboard Erik's private jet, looking out the window wishing she had her cell phone. She had no idea where Emily was or when she would arrive in

Italy. Ryker knew who she really was, she'd been kidnapped and she couldn't even warn her twin. Or beg for forgiveness.

They'd been in the air for several hours. Plenty of time to contemplate her situation.

Whoever Erik was, he had money. Power. Big, scary, Viking-looking hunks crawling all over the place. The few words he'd said to Katy since she'd been whisked away in the car gave her no clue as to who he was. He had the same strange, not quite familiar accent that Ryker did. Erik signaled one of his Guardians to come over.

Erik sat in the seat facing her this time. "Can you bring me a whiskey, please? Ms. Toure? Anything for you? White wine? A spritzer? Sparkling water? Are you hungry?"

She shouldn't, she really shouldn't, but she could not get the image of those dragons out of her head. Either she was seeing things, or the world no longer made sense. "I'll take a double shot of tequila."

Erik grinned at her as the large man left them to get the drinks. If she wasn't totally in love with Ryker, then Erik could definitely turn a girl's head. The man was drop-dead gorgeous. Even if he had kidnapped her.

"Now, Ms. Toure, or may I call you Emily?"

Holy shit. He thought she was Emily? Of course he did. She was an idiot.

What the hell had her wonderful, amazing, dear, dear sister gotten her into now?

She took a deep breath. Mentally reviewed the twin swap rules again. Gave Erik a super fake smile. "Sure. Emily is fine." Might as well try to appease him for the moment. Be polite. Give Ryker and the Guardians time to come after her. Because they would. She was sure of it. This guy was on borrowed time.

"Thank you, Emily. You may call me Erik."

"Okay." The giant Viking set the double shot of tequila in front of her, glass perfectly rimmed with salt, along with a fresh slice of lime. She settled a generous number of the salt crystals onto her tongue and gulped down the tequila, grateful for the instant warmth spreading in her gut, and ignored the lime. This was not the time.

Erik sipped his whiskey on ice and watched her in silence.

Finally, tired of waiting, she spoke first. "Why did you kidnap me, Erik? What do you want?"

"I want the truth."

Well, that was fine with her. As long as she knew what the truth was. "All right."

"How did Ryker recruit you for this contract?"

Oh hell. She had no idea and, per twin swapping rules, shouldn't lie. "I don't recall exactly, but I have a lot of contacts all over the world. Pretty sure someone I know mentioned a website."

"I see. And what, exactly, were the contents of this posting? What attracted you to the job?"

Knowing Emily, that answer was easy. "Money. My mother has a lot of medical bills, and we didn't have a way to pay them."

"We being you and your identical twin sister, Katy?"

"Yes." He knew her name. Knew Emily had an identical twin. Katy shivered. What else did he know?

"Excellent." Erik motioned one of the giant blond men forward with a slight wave of his wrist. The man came forward and handed Erik a business-sized manila envelope.

Erik opened the flap and withdrew a stack of paperwork that looked like legal contracts. After a quick glance at God only knew what details, he handed them to Katy.

At first glance, the paperwork appeared to be the same contract Vector and Ryker had tried to get her to sign in his office. Same gorgeous dragon symbol at the top. Same type of paper. Without reading a word, she looked from the paperwork to Erik's expectant face. "What is this?"

"This, Ms. Toure, is a contract with exactly the same terms offered to you by Ryker, but for ten times the payment. I will also repay the advance you and your sister used to pay for your mother's rehabilitation facility and private nursing."

"What?" Katy nearly came unglued. Ten times the

money? Hadn't Emily said her deal was a lot of money? Coming from Emily, that could only have meant millions. And Erik was willing to pay ten times that amount? What the hell?

Erik leaned forward, clearly gaining confidence with each moment of her silence. "As I said, the terms are identical. We will be legally married at once. I will introduce you as queen of my clan at an inaugural ball. We can tell the other clans Ryker did not properly woo you.

Once we're married, you will provide the clan with at least two children within the first five years via IVF; no sexual contact between us is required. You, as the mother of my children, will be cared for by the clan. My top financial advisors will take care of the children's assets, of course, until the eldest child comes of age at twenty-five. You will have a beautiful home— several, actually—more money than you can imagine deposited into your personal account, and two beautiful children to love without the problem of an irritating husband around. I assume this pleases you?"

Dumbfounded, Katy could only think of one question. "Children need their fathers. Why wouldn't you be around?"

"Just like Ryker, I await the executioner."

Erik held out a pen. With shaking fingers, Katy took it from him and settled back in her seat.

"Two children?"

"Ms. Toure, of course I would be thrilled if you

decided to carry additional heirs, but I am honoring the original agreement offered to you by Ryker. Should you wish to have additional children after my death, I am sure the frozen embryos will remain viable for some time."

IVF? Frozen embryos?

Katy's head began to pound. She rubbed her temples to ease the pain as she considered Erik's bizarre proposition, or rather, Ryker's deal with Emily. Her sister agreed to marry Ryker, but never sleep with him? A marriage in name only? Have his babies via IVF? And stay in Italy, at his estate, *for twenty-five years*?

Katy's head spun dizzily. Ryker was going to be *executed*?

She was going to vomit, the tequila choosing that very moment to rise from her stomach like a fire snake eating its way up her throat.

Unbuckling her lap belt, she stood and made her way to the toilet in the back of the plane. Luckily, even private jets were laid out in a way that made the small room easy to find. Locked inside, she stared at herself in the mirror and tried to recognize the woman staring back at her.

Her hair was still gorgeous, the hairstyle Ryker's servants had spent over an hour creating, perfect. Her make-up had been artfully applied. She looked beautiful. The engagement ring on her finger sparkled like black fire surrounded by a ring of starlight. The dress she wore was unlike anything she had ever imagined. It hugged every curve, made her look...like a queen.

Mia Regina.

My queen. Not a charming endearment. A freaking *title*.

Fumbling with the water spouts, she managed to turn it on and splash a bit of cold water on her cheeks and neck.

Inaugural ball? Like the event at Ryker's estate tonight? The people, all looking like they'd come straight from a fashion catalog? The pendant worn by Ryker's mother? The crown?

"Emily, what have you done?" she whispered to the mirror image of herself. If she had her cell phone, she would call her twin this instant and curse her into next week. But she had no phone. No identification. No passport. No money. And everyone on this jet thought she was Emily Toure, future wife of Ryker. Future mother of his children.

For a price.

"No." She stared the woman who looked exactly like Emily in the eye and told her again. "No. I'm not doing this. Not even for you."

Decision made, Katy made sure she didn't look as unsettled as she felt and walked back to stand next to her seat. The contract and pen rested in Erik's lap.

"I am sorry, Erik. But I cannot accept your offer."

"You drive a hard bargain, Ms. Toure." He smiled as he spoke, clearly unperturbed. He stood and held out the paperwork. "I'll make it twenty million and one child. Please, Ms. Toure. My clan, too, has given up hope, and the dragon chains will not hold us much longer."

Straightening her shoulders, Katy made a decision.

"Erik, please, sit. I have a lot of questions. And then I have a story to tell you as well."

"Ask. I will tell you anything, *min dronning*."

"What does that mean?"

"My queen."

14

Monday, Island of Sørøya, Norway

ursing the daylight, Ryker ground his teeth and shifted the car Vector had acquired for them into high gear, the tires squealing as he took a sharp curve. Half a day to heal, just over three hours in the jet to Hasvik, and then a half-hour drive. Erik certainly knew how to hide from humans. His estate was on the clifflike shores of Noregr, although the humans had renamed the land Norway. His castle had been built between two small villages on the island of Sørøya. The entire island was home to just over a thousand humans.

"Send us over the cliff into that fucking ice water and you'll have to wait another day to heal before you can get to her." Vector's blasé protest of his driving had the desired effect, and Ryker slowed to a reasonable speed.

Well, reasonable for a dragon who would have much preferred flying directly to the castle in full view. Staying hidden from the humans was not something his dragon cared about at the moment.

Ryker snarled. "I am going to disembowel him. Tear out his throat. Slash him to pieces and bury him alive."

"He's a king, old friend." Crammed into the back seat, knees nearly to his chin, Alrik's amusement served to irritate.

"He took my mate."

"Technically he did not. He escorted a female business associate from your estate," Vector pointed out. "No one knows she is your true mate, not even the lady in question."

Ryker's dragon roared in fury at Vector's truth. He winced, his head about to split in two with his dragon's anger. "Do not speak of it. I am barely keeping him at bay."

"Even with the dragon chains?" Alrik asked, and it was not lost on Ryker that he was not asking as a friend but in his role as executioner.

"Yes."

Alrik sighed. "Well then, hurry the fuck up."

Ryker clenched his fists around the wheel, increasing the vehicle's speed once more. The car's mapping system indicated they were still twenty minutes away on winding roads that passed nothing but seaside cliffs and empty countryside.

And it was cold. Wet. The air was soggy with a mix of rain and sea spray so thick Ryker's face and neck were coated with it.

"Fuck this," He slammed on the brakes and pulled the car to the side of the road.

"You can't. It's broad daylight," Vector pointed out.

"You may not regain control of him." Alrik's statement about his dragon was more worrisome than breaking the rule about not revealing themselves to the humans. If someone wanted to punish Ryker for risking discovery, they could try, but he had won his place as king centuries ago and no one dared challenge him for leadership. He was the fastest, toughest, most dangerous dragon in the clan, and he was not spending another moment driving the slow human vehicle when he could be there in a quarter of the time by flying straight to King Erik's estate.

Ryker opened the door and stood on the open road. There were no cars, no humans for miles. He had to applaud Erik; the king's northern estate was remote, desolate, and built on the cliffs for easy defense. Perfect for a dragon. Ryker's estate in Italy had once been the same, but that had been in ancient times, before modern cities, and humans invaded every bit of exposed earth.

The thought enraged his dragon even more. They were guardians of the planet, of nature, of all life, yet the billions of humans had overcome their best efforts. Now the dragons operated from the shadows, doing what little could be done to save humanity from itself.

Humans need to die, Dragon insisted.

Your mate is human, old one.

Katy can live. The rest need to die. Like Erik. I will destroy Erik.

Erik is a dragon.

He is a dead dragon.

Fuck. His dragon was in a bad mood. And Ryker was about to turn him loose.

Vector and Alrik both climbed out of the car on the passenger side and looked over the low rooftop. Vector crossed his arms and leaned over the top of the car. "You sure about this?"

"My dragon is very sure," Ryker answered.

"That's what I'm afraid of."

Alrik grinned and slapped Vector on the back. "You worry too much. Erik is an ancient, nearly as old as Ryker. He can take care of himself."

With a growl, Ryker's dragon took over and initiated the change. Seconds later a shimmering black dragon three times the size of the sports car stood on the road, testing his wings.

Vector sighed. "We'll meet you there. In the car."

Dragon answered, his telepathic voice a loud boom in both his companions' minds. *No. By the time you get there, we'll be gone. She comes with me.*

"This isn't your territory. Where will you take her?"

Dragon would have laughed if he weren't so eager to get to his mate. He'd been alive for centuries. Explored every part of the world. He knew the air and the mountains, the forests and the rivers. Earth, all of her, was his home. *Airport. Tomorrow. Dawn.*

"Fine. Don't be late, Ryker. If you aren't back in control and at that airport with Katy by sunrise, it won't be a friend coming for you," Alrik warned.

Dragon didn't bother to respond before he launched into the skies. If his mate refused him, he would welcome the executioner's blade.

Deep within, the human part of him agreed. One way or another, the chains must come off. Their torment would end.

* * *

aty: *it's me, katy. new number. long story. where are you?*

Katy: *why aren't you answering me? Whatever you do, don't go to the palazzo. call me.*

aty sipped at her breakfast tea and tried to ignore the awkward silence at the large table. Erik and the twelve Guardians— which he'd told her were other dragon shape-shifters in his clan—sat around the table packing away food like starving giants. Erik had eaten little and continued to study her with a pensive expression on his face.

What was he thinking? She'd asked him hundreds of questions, and he'd answered them all. She wasn't quite sure she believed him, wouldn't think twice about dismissing his claims if she hadn't seen those dragons fighting over the water with her own eyes.

She glanced at each person at the table in turn. The Guardians on the private jet knew everything, had overheard her discussion with Erik. Her confession.

When she told Erik about the plan to switch places with Emily, he had actually thrown back his head and laughed. "You think you can fool a dragon so easily?"

Even now, she stared at him, irritated. "Well, your kingship, we didn't know about dragons."

What a freaking mess.

"I want to see it," Katy blurted before she could change her mind.

"See what, my dear?"

"Your dragon. I want to watch you shift, or whatever you called it, into your dragon."

All movement at the table ceased as if by magic, every single one of them looked like they'd turned into stone with her words.

Erik turned his head to look out one of the many floor-to-ceiling windows that looked out over a large stone courtyard, took so long in answering that Katy started to squirm. It was the only movement at the table.

"Very well. Come with me." Erik walked away from the table and out onto the courtyard through a large set of enormous double doors. Knowing what she knew now, she wondered if the doors were wide enough to accommodate a dragon.

Outside, the cold wind coming off the water cut through her borrowed jeans and sweater. One of Erik's many servants had brought her a selection of night-gowns, clothing, and shoes upon their arrival at the estate late last night. Katy had pulled on the warmest pair of flannel pajamas she could find in the stack of offerings and crawled into bed.

Erik's castle was far north. As in, the-air-smelled-like-ice far. The ocean waves below crashed against the rocks menacingly, completely opposite the warm waters outside Ryker's estate in Italy. The air itself was damp and cold and made her bones ache.

She missed Ryker. Which was stupid, because he'd been lying to her the entire time. He was, technically, still engaged to marry Emily. And he was a shape-shifting beast who wanted to impregnate her sister via IVF and then kill himself. Or, have someone called The Executioner kill him. That's what Erik called the man.

No, not man. Elf. Not only was she supposed to believe dragons were real, but dark elves, light elves, werewolves. She'd stopped Erik there, her brain refusing to compute.

"I've totally lost it; that's the only explanation for all

of this," Katy mumbled under her breath as she walked behind Erik. Finally, he stopped in the center of the stone courtyard.

"Please, step back. Once I have shifted, you may approach. Slowly. My dragon knows and has agreed to allow you to see him."

Was she supposed to thank the dragon? She had no idea. Backing away, her heart racing like a rabbit's, she kept going until Erik nodded that she was at a safe distance.

"Do not run, Katy. My dragon loves to hunt."

Was that supposed to be funny? "Not funny."

Erik chuckled and then closed his eyes.

For a few seconds nothing happened. Then everything happened at once. The man she knew as Erik, in his much more casual pants and turtleneck sweater, shimmered like a phantom before a strange light blocked her view of him. Almost like fog, only made of light instead of mist. She couldn't see anything for the space of a heartbeat. And then?

Katy gasped. Standing before her was a dragon made of silver, his scales sparkling like small, interlocking pieces of chrome on his back, darkening to a more matte stainless-steel color under his chest and the bottom sides of his wings. Only Erik's warning kept her feet planted on the ground, every instinct she had screaming at her to run.

Eric's claws were black and longer than her arms, the tips sharp as knife blades. His eyes were bright blue sapphires that sparkled like brilliantly cut gemstones with a dark, slanted pupil in the center.

Not human. Nothing even close to human.

Dragon eyes.

"You're beautiful." The words were honest, but Katy's shock was real. She hadn't been imagining those flying creatures out over the water, like she'd half convinced herself at least a dozen times on the way here. They were real.

Dragons were real.

I am dragon.

The voice came from inside her mind, and she held her breath, listening for more.

You may approach, human.

So, it wasn't her imagination then. This creature was actually speaking to her with some kind of... what? Telepathic power? Telepathy? How was that possible? And in her native language?

She answered her own question. Because he was a dragon. Magic. Right?

Moving forward slowly, Katy completely forgot about the cold, her half-broken heart, Ryker, marriage contracts, and her sister. The world faded away as she approached the most beautiful creature she'd ever seen or even imagined. Hand outstretched, she was shocked when the mighty beast, at least four times her height, bent down low and rested his head on the stones so she could reach his face.

The teeth and jaw were a bit too much for her to

handle, so she walked a few steps closer and reached for the spot below the dragon's ear where she knew her neighbor's cat liked to be scratched. Her fingertips came to rest on the dragon's cheek, and she grinned as heat flowed into her from the contact.

"Do you breathe fire?" she whispered, unsure of her voice. Erik was, after all, a creature of pure fantasy. Magical. Legendary.

In response, the dragon made a huffing sound, and small flames shot from the dragon's snout as if she had asked a stupid question.

"I've never met a dragon before. I didn't mean to offend."

The dragon leaned toward her again, bumping her hand just like a demanding cat wanting attention.

Proceed, human.

"Of course, Your Majesty." Katy couldn't keep the nervous giggle out of her voice as she rubbed the dragon's cheek, right below his ear. For about a minute he held perfectly still. A low rumble began, moving through the stones and up into the soles of Katy's feet.

Was he purring? Or maybe rumbling like the elephants did, the tone so low human ears couldn't pick up the sound?

After several minutes the dragon lifted its head and stretched to his full height. *Not mate.*

Katy had to agree. "No, I'm not."

Erik wants to make a bargain.

Uh-oh. What was she supposed to say to that? "He does."

I do not. I feel dragon magic in you. You belong to another.

"Dragon magic?"

Dragon looked down at her, his blue eyes hypnotically beautiful.

You are true mate. He will come.

She wanted to pretend she didn't know who Erik's dragon was talking about, but she knew. Ryker. Ryker would come for her. She'd known, deep in her bones, that he would come for her, and the truth of that had kept her from panicking when Erik kidnapped her. She'd known. That didn't mean she wasn't mad as hell and hurting and feeling stupid and betrayed.

They stared at one another for long seconds, and Katy felt like she had made a new friend, or friends, in both Erik and his dragon.

"You really are beautiful."

The dragon nodded its head as if to say thank you and reached forward with one wing.

Fly with me.

What? Fly? On a dragon? She wanted to, kind of, but the fear of freezing to death warred with the fear of falling off. Still, how many people had the chance to ride a freaking dragon? With a grin, she reached out to touch the soft edge of the dragon's wing. It was softer than his face, like warm, smooth silk.

A roar thundered through the sky, and Erik's

dragon looked up at the same time Katy did to see a dark shadow coming at them like an arrow out of the sky.

Get back!

Erik's dragon used his wing to lift her and throw her toward the building. She was flailing, flying backward through the air, bracing for a very painful landing when a pair of strong arms plucked her from thin air and settled her gently on her feet. One of Erik's Guardians stood next to her, scowling at his king.

Erik's dragon launched himself into the air with an answering roar that rattled Katy's rib cage.

A huge black dragon reached out with sharp talons and struck at the silver, their bodies tangling above the courtyard before both beasts crashed to the ground, ripping and thrashing at one another.

She looked at the Guardian standing next to her. "Why aren't you doing something?"

"My king forbids interference. He wants the fight."

Katy clenched her fists. She wanted to strangle the Guardian. Strangle Erik. Strangle the black beast that she somehow knew was Ryker. "You're all idiots."

The Guardian crossed his arms and moved to block her body from the fight but said nothing.

"Get out of my way," she fumed.

"No. You are to be protected." He turned to her with flames dancing inside his eyes like candles. "Stand back. Do not challenge me."

That was the last straw. She was seething mad.

"Take your fire eyes and shove them where the sun don't shine, Mr. Guardian Man. Get out of my way."

The Guardian looked down at her for a few seconds. Katy glared right back.

He laughed and the transformation was shocking. He was...gorgeous. Every single one of these damn dragon-clan people were too damn good-looking to be real. "You are a true mate. Go then. Take your dragon with you before my king decides to do something stupid."

"Like what?"

"End his torment. There are only two ways a dragon can die. The executioner's blade, or in battle with another dragon."

Katy looked up to see the silver and black dragons breathing fire at one another as they plummeted toward the water, neither letting go. The ultimate game of chicken.

"Can they drown?"

"No. They are of the earth itself. Your dragon is a king, Katy. The oldest among us."

"He's not my dragon." Katy denied the truth, but she knew it was a lie. Even now she could somehow feel the black dragon's heartbeat, his rage, his fire. The sensation of warmth spread through her entire body, made her breasts heavy and her core ignite with desire. Memories of their time together filled her mind as the familiar heat surged in her veins.

Was that what she'd felt that night in his arms? The

heated, orgasmic, mind-numbing pleasure she'd had in Ryker's bed? Dragon magic? Was that what Erik's dragon had sensed in her? Had Ryker marked her somehow? Made her off-limits to other dragons?

The thought should upset her, but somehow the idea that a magical bond existed between her and Ryker was reassuring. Ryker had known the whole time who she was. Knew he was making love to her that first time, not Emily. He'd said as much at the ball.

And he belonged to her. What that meant, she had no idea, but was overcome with the need to find out.

She moved to push past the Guardian.

"Stay back!" He lifted her from her feet and shoved her several steps behind him just as Ryker and Erik, still battling in their dragon forms, crashed to the courtyard on their sides, claws and tails thrashing and ripping one another to pieces. Blood sprayed in every direction, soaking the cobblestones and turning the courtyard from a beautiful, serene oasis to a nightmare scene from the worst kind of horror movie.

Ryker had his jaws locked around Eric's throat just as Eric had a talon pressed to Ryker's long dragon neck. They remained locked together, unmoving. Bleeding. Each a hair's breadth from death.

Katy ran around the Guardian and walked straight toward both dragons, her heart about to jump out of her throat as two pairs of eyes locked onto her movements. One blue sapphire, the other black diamond.

Neither dragon moved an inch, unrelenting in their death grip on the other.

"Ryker, let him go. Right now. He didn't hurt me."

The ground under her feet rumbled again.

Took you. Kill him.

The voice in her head this time was distinctly different from that of Erik's dragon, and she knew she was speaking, for the very first time, to Ryker's dragon. Her dragon. The one who thought she was his true mate, whatever that meant. "Let. Him. Go. Now."

Inside her mind, the silver dragon issued a warning. *Stand back, human. He is in a killing rage. I will kill him. Protect you.*

"No!" Unable to bear the thought of Ryker's death, Katy ran toward the two dragons. Locked together as they were, she didn't have far to climb to reach the place where the Ryker's teeth were locked around Eric's silver throat. With shaking hands, she reached toward Ryker's jaw and pulled with every ounce of force she possessed. "Let. Him. Go."

Foolish, Eric rumbled.

Dangerous, growled Ryker.

"Stop fighting!" she shouted furiously at both of them.

Eric's dragon slowly, deliberately lifted his claw from Ryker's bleeding neck. Once the pressure was gone, Ryker opened his maw to allow Eric to break free.

Katy rolled to the ground as the two dragons

stepped back from one another, dripping blood, eyes locked on each other's movements. They circled her like warring tigers separated by a referee.

"Enough. Ryker, I want to talk to you. Now. You have some explaining to do."

Right in front of her eyes the black dragon disappeared in the magical fog of light she'd first seen with Erik, replaced by the man she knew, the man whose touch made her forget her own name. The man who treated her like a queen. The man she'd fallen in love with despite of the lies, the deception. She had even betrayed her own sister for him.

Ryker watched her, his chest heaving. Behind her she felt the magic of Erik's change, but her focus was on only one man. "Ryker."

He walked toward her, lifting the golden necklace, the Elven dragon chains he always wore, over his head, tossed the chain to the side and scooped her into his arms, cradling her against his chest. "Are you hurt?"

"No."

Ryker lifted his head to where Erik stood behind her. "For that, I will let you live."

Erik growled. "My dragon senses that you have marked her but not yet claimed her. She is vulnerable to attack. Take care of your mate, Ryker. She will spark hope among our people. We cannot afford to lose her."

Ryker lowered his chin to acknowledge Erik's words, then turned and walked to the edge of the courtyard. Far below them, white-capped water churned against the cliff.

"Ryker? That's a long—"

Ryker leaped off the balcony.

Katy screamed.

15

Dragon:

The black dragon's chest pressed to Katy's cheek. His talons cradled her like precious cargo. For the first few minutes, she'd closed her eyes in panic. Once the fear gave way to wonder, she watched the land flow beneath them like a river as the dragon carried her...somewhere. She had no idea where he was taking her, but he wouldn't hurt her. That was the only thing she was sure of.

If he'd wanted to kill her, she'd given him the perfect opportunity while crawling up his neck to pull at the dragon's jaw. Like that would have worked. *I can't bench press a hundred pounds on my best day.*

"Where are we going?" She spoke aloud, experience over the last few hours proof that the dragon could hear her perfectly, for she had received the same one-word reply to every question she asked during the flight.

Mine.

Katy's lips twitched. She wasn't quite ready to outright laugh at the dragon, but she was getting close. "Okay. Mine. Mine. Mine. But where are we going?"

The dragon ignored her. There was literally nothing she could do but wait.

An hour could have passed, or three, she had no idea, enthralled by the most exciting ride of her life. Slowly, Ryker began doing lazy flips and turns for no other reason she could fathom except it made her scream and laugh. Katy suspected more than once that the big black dragon was trying to impress her, as if just being a dragon wouldn't do the trick.

Ryker slowly spiraled down toward the ground. She peeked out from between his claws and spotted a tiny cottage sitting atop a cliff overlooking a vast expanse of ocean with nothing else around as far as she could see.

"Is this place yours?"

Yes. Ryker owns. Mine.

Okay, so Ryker owned a tiny cottage by the sea. And he was a dragon. A gorgeous black dragon the color of sparkling black diamonds on top and deep obsidian beneath.

"Are all dragons this beautiful?" she asked. "And you're not allowed to say 'mine' again." The long ride with the dragon had worked its own kind of magic, and her fear of him was entirely gone. Well, mostly gone.

The dragon preened. *Dragon beautiful to mate.*

Katy laughed out loud this time at his smug reply. Dragons, she was discovering, could be charming when they chose.

Smell other Draquonir magic on mate. Remove smell. Mine.

"What does that mean?"

Katy looked down at herself, looked at the jeans and sweater Erik loaned her along with a pair of very comfortable shoes. Nothing out of the ordinary there. She twisted her upper body so that she could check behind her. Nope. Still nothing.

The dragon didn't elaborate as he flew lower and lower before landing just outside the cottage door. He opened his claw slowly, and she slid down his finger and talon like it was a child's slide. The moment her feet touched the ground, Ryker transformed into his human self. "You reek of Erik's magic."

"I'm sorry?"

With a grunt that sounded like he was in pain, he took her elbow and gently escorted her toward the cottage. The door opened, and he pulled her inside. Built from peat or sod, the structure gave her the sense that it was hundreds of years old. Maybe older. "What is this place?"

"I was born here."

"When?"

"We didn't keep records back then. A long time ago." He walked toward one corner of the room where a large, claw-foot tub rested next to the wall. There was no curtain and a hand pump for water. Ryker filled the tub.

Katy's heart thundered. "How long ago? I mean, how old are you, exactly?"

He looked up at her, really looked at her for the first time since she'd discovered who and what he really was. She saw something in his eyes he'd never allowed her to see before. Pain. Fear. Regret.

"I lost track at twelve hundred."

"Years?"

"Yes. I stopped counting after that."

"Oh my God." Katy looked around the cottage where Ryker had been born and took in the ancient, heavy wooden beams that held the ceiling. An old-fashioned stone firepit and chimney stood in one corner of the room with a bed in the opposite corner. The space was smaller than a studio flat back home and gave off a rustic feeling. A single dusty oil lantern hung from a hook next to the fireplace. It was daylight now, the door stood open behind them, but she could easily imagine how cozy the small cottage would be at night with nothing but firelight and candles to push back the darkness.

No sooner had the thought crossed her mind than Ryker waved a hand and closed the door, shutting out the cold. He turned to the firepit next. Katy gasped as a spark flew from his finger straight into the dry kindling left behind, burning hot and fast until the logs caught fire, flickering and crackling, no doubt for the first time in many years. Soft shadows danced along the wall and the scent of pine filled the small cottage.

She had no idea what to say as Ryker filled a tub with water, then tested the temperature with his fingertips. Leaning down, he placed both hands inside. They glowed black, like sparkling glitter beneath the water until hot steam curled languidly around them.

"I hope that's for you. You're a mess." And he was. Covered in blood and gashes from his fight with Erik, she wasn't sure how he was still on his feet.

"This is nothing. And no, this is for you, mate. Dragon cannot wait any longer to claim you."

Katy frowned; her brow creased in confusion. "I don't understand. What does that mean, exactly? To be claimed by a dragon?"

"Trust me." Ryker's tone was seductive now, his eyes growing darker as he closed the distance between them. He lifted his palms to pull her to his side, her cheek settling against his chest. "I would never hurt you, my mate."

Warmth spread throughout her limbs. Desire. A languid sense of safety, of being cared for, protected, filled her heart. She was tired of fighting. Tired of struggling to survive. Tired of being alone and in pain.

Katy wrapped her arms around his waist and squeezed. She didn't ever want him to let her go. Didn't want to return to the daily struggle she'd faced before she knew him, alone and lonely. Fighting the whole world by herself every time her sister went off traipsing around the globe, leaving Katy to take care of everything.

She closed her eyes and breathed him in as the warmth turned to crackling flames. With a gasp, she looked down to see her clothing disintegrate before her eyes, black flames consuming the material yet leaving her skin untouched. Magic. She shivered, half afraid of the flames and half in awe.

"Much better." Ryker lifted her naked body to his chest then stepped into the water, his eyes sparkling with mischief as his own clothes disappeared as well.

"You can make clothes?"

"We are dragons. Made from the magic of Earth itself. We can manipulate anything that is part of us. The elements. Earth. Air. Fire. Water. Spirit. You were covered in Erik's magic, the clothing you wore created by his dragonfire. I cannot stand to sense his energy or catch his scent on you. It makes my dragon insane."

Mine. The loud, insistent voice she'd heard repeatedly during the flight burst into her mind in agreement.

Ryker laughed as he lowered them both into the steaming water. "See? I told you."

Katy relaxed in his arms and let Ryker have his way with her. He was gentle, soaping and rinsing her hair before running his hands over every inch of her body.

His touch was careful, tender, and not at all what she wanted right now.

Turning in his arms, she pressed her naked breasts to his chest and wrapped her arms around his neck, pleased to see that nearly all his wounds had healed. Taking the soap from his hand, she washed the remaining signs of battle from his body and kissed him. Hard. Deep. Demanding.

He answered in kind, taking control of the kiss, his arms moving to hold her closer. Tighter.

No! Mine!

"Damn it, Dragon." Ryker tore his lips from hers and pressed his forehead to hers, staring into her eyes. "He is tired of waiting. I cannot control him. I took off my dragon chains."

"Is he going to hurt me?"

Dragon's telepathic denial came the same instant Ryker responded.

Never.

"Okay. Then I'm ready to meet your dragon. Officially. As long as he promises not to fly away with me again, especially when I'm naked."

With a grin, Ryker stood, lifting her from the tub as he rose. The cooler air in the cottage made her shiver. A moment later she was covered in magical black fire. When it was gone, she was wearing some sort of gown, similar to the one she'd worn to the ball. Black. Shimmering. Beautiful. Her hair and skin were dry, her feet covered in thick slippers.

Ryker, still naked himself, set her on her feet, took her hand and walked her outside until they stood looking out over the cliffs. Together they watched the seagulls fly, darting into the water to catch fish. The surf was so far below them it was a quiet, rhythmic, peaceful sound. Katy remained quiet as Ryker looked pensively out at the sea far below.

Finally, he turned to her. "Long ago I dreamed of finding my true mate and bringing her here, to my ancient home, to claim her." Ryker looked deeply into her eyes. "I love you, Katy. I am yours. Dragon is yours. If you'll have us."

Katy took in the sight of her gorgeous, muscled god of a lover looking at her with the stars themselves in his eyes. No one had ever looked at her like that; like she was everything. Her heart melted.

The magical blur she knew meant Ryker was changing into his dragon form filled her vision, and then it was just her and the dragon, staring at one another.

"Dragon."

Mine.

"I don't know what that means."

The creature did not answer with words, but with visions. She saw herself enveloped in black flames, the magic becoming part of her. Then, a new life form growing within her, black dragonfire growing more powerful with every beat of his or her tiny heart.

Her dragon's magic. Hers and Ryker's.

"My children will be like you? What you are?"

I choose you. My soul. My power. Yours. I protect. Love. You become immortal. Dangerous. Powerful. Magic. My children. Mine.

"Why? Why me?"

Mine.

Katy allowed her question to fade away. Did the why matter when she wanted Ryker with every cell in her body? When she knew he wanted her? Would it be so bad to have their future children be powerful, immortal, magical creatures? Protected by not only this dragon, but an entire clan watching over them? They would be beautiful and strong. Fierce. Unafraid.

Something she realized she'd never been, not a single day in her life.

She looked into the dragon's eyes. He watched her, waited for her to make a choice. "What if I say no? What happens then?"

We go.

She saw his intention clearly. He would carry her to safety and then disappear from her life. Forever.

She knew what he truly meant, thanks to Erik. He would sacrifice himself to the executioner's blade. Some Dark Elf would stab him in the heart, and the black, magical blade would take the dragon's life.

Tears gathering in her eyes, she watched in growing wonder as the dragon settled along the ground just as Erik's dragon had done. His large, black head nearly within reach, his eye resigned and weary.

"Ryker." She stepped forward and wrapped as much of the dragon's head in a hug as she could manage, leaned her entire body against him. She rubbed his cheek and the ridge near his eye, smiling when he rewarded her with a deep rumble she felt not just through the ground, but everywhere she pressed against him. "I am yours, Dragon."

The dragon shuddered at her words. Slowly he lifted his head and turned to look at her.

She stood perfectly still as the dragon's jaw opened, fire visible in the back of his throat. If he was going to roast her, there was nothing she could do about it now.

"Go ahead, Dragon."

The dragon took a long, deep breath and then... fire. Black flames. Magic sparkling all around her. Her body tingled, caressed by a hundred unseen hands, her very insides flooded with warmth and health.

She breathed deeply, every hurt, disappeared. Every scar, vanished. Life itself flooded her cells, and she felt the earth in her bones, sensed the very stars. The wind wrapped around her in a gentle hello, and she knew she would never walk alone again. She was dragon, one with all life. One with the earth and the stars, the mountains and the trees. Every bird in the sky spoke to her. The wind itself whispered in her ear.

Deeper still, she knew the moment the dragon's magic touched her womb, left a spark that would ensure any future children would be dragon as well.

The black flames wove around her. Eternal. Dragonfire. She raised her arms to the sky as a feeling of joyous freedom filled her being.

Ryker appeared, strode toward her inside the flames. He was naked, his body hard and ready.

She reached for him. Leaped into his embrace. "What about the flames? Why didn't the dragon stop them?"

Ryker threw back his head and laughed with pure joy. "The flames are coming from you now, love. They're coming from you."

16

Ryker:

*R*yker nearly staggered as he shifted from dragon to human form. The relentless pain he'd endured for centuries was gone.

Because of her. Katy. His mate.

Dragon agreed. *Fire. Mine. Powerful.*

Ryker didn't argue, the smug sense of happiness the dragon was feeling matching his own. The dragon chains were gone. The magic that had been building, festering, gathering into a storm inside him with no outlet had been tempered. Katy had saved him. Accepted part of his dragon's magic, his soul. Given Dragon the outlet he needed to remain in control of his mind.

On the hilltop opposite him, Katy raised her hands

to the heavens, her body surrounded by black flames that flew around her in a whirlwind larger than the cottage.

No wonder he could barely walk. The shock to his system was intense. His agony, the relentless fire and fury that was his dragon's magic, the constant struggle to contain the power building and building within his cells...gone. The dragon was quiet. Content. For the first time in his adult life, Ryker was at peace.

All because of the beautiful, giving woman before him. She'd accepted his dragon, accepted him.

His dragon stirred as Ryker stared.

Mine.

Yes, Dragon. She is ours now.

If the dragon could have looked smug, Ryker had no doubt he would. But since the beast was locked inside him at the moment, all he could do was repeat the word Ryker was thinking.

Mine. Mine. Mine.

Shut up, beast. I'm working on it.

Apparently satisfied that Ryker was working toward their shared goal of being as close as possible to their mate, Dragon quieted, leaving Ryker's very male needs to drive him closer. And closer.

As if on cue, Katy turned to face him as he walked to her. His mate. His life. His soul. She was everything.

She ran to him and leaped into his arms. He wrapped her up tight, vowed he would never let her go.

"What about the flames? Why didn't the dragon stop them?"

Pure happiness flooded him, and he laughed at her question. She had no idea what she was now. The extent of her power. The gift the dragon had given her. But she would learn, and Ryker would spend the rest of forever teaching her what it meant to be the true mate of a Draquonir. A queen among his people. The chosen female of an ancient dragon.

"The flames are coming from you now, love. They're coming from you."

"What?" She looked around them, eyes growing larger and larger as the truth became clear to her. "That's me?"

"That's us."

Her head snapped back, her brown eyes alight with their own power now. Her connection to the dragon was strong. "Ryker, Emily is going to be so mad at me for stealing you."

"Hush, love. She was not meant to be mine. She will understand. She will be happy for you."

"But the payment."

"I already paid for the rest of your mother's rehabilitation. I have sent Guardians to bring both your sister and your mother to the estate in time for the wedding."

"Wedding?"

"Dragon and I have claimed you, but I assumed you would want to follow your own traditions? In America I believe you like to have a large white dress and your family in attendance as I vow to love you forever."

"You love me now?"

"More than life, female. More than life itself."

"I love you, too. But technically you belong to my sister."

Ryker laughed. "I torched that damn contract the same day you signed it. Any child we share will be made the old-fashioned way."

Looking mischievous now, Katy lifted her lips to his and wiggled her backside in his hands, taking advantage of the fact that he still held her off the ground, her legs wrapped around his waist. The black flames still danced around them, but they were smaller now, the tempting bite of magic racing along his skin as he held her. "The old-fashioned way? I don't believe I know what that is."

He couldn't wait any longer. Taking her mouth with his, he took what he wanted, what he needed. Her. Her taste. Her smell. The small whimper at the back of her throat.

With a whisper of magic he removed her clothing, her heated skin pressed to his, black dragonfire dancing between them, around them, sealing them together in a dance older than time itself. Older than dragons.

With one quick movement of his hands on her hips, he lifted her into position and lowered her onto his hard length, sending an extra burst of dragonfire into her as he took her.

Her orgasm slammed into her, her hot core clenching down on his body like a fist.

"Ryker..." His name was a moan on her lips as he pumped into her body, taking her over and over again.

He lowered her to the ground, calling forth a bed of soft grass and flowers to cradle his mate's back. He followed her down, body buried deep as black fire leaped from her hand to his back, his back to her hip, flickering and dancing around them as if it had a mind of its own.

Perhaps it did. Ryker had never had a mate before. Understood little of what would come in the years ahead. He would need to rely on his dragon and his instincts to take care of their mate.

And care for her he would. Honor her. Worship her body and soul. Cherish and protect her soft heart. She was a treasure, and every legend that existed knew how vehemently dragons guarded their treasure.

She arched her back, lifting her hips, driving him deeper as she used his hair to pull his head to hers. To place her lips on his. To make her own claim.

"You're mine, Ryker. Mine. You can't take this back."

His kiss silenced her. His hips pumped into her with a driving rhythm as he pushed dragonfire into her body, swallowed her screams of pleasure with his kiss.

He held on as long as he could, his need for her driving all thought and reason from his mind. Her tight heat gripped his cock, driving him wild. Her flame, the black flame that would seal them together forever, moved over and through his body like a lover's caress, Katy's sensuality, her passion, her love touching him in every cell. Healing him. Making him whole.

He gave himself to the pleasure of her body and knew he was home.

EPILOGUE

Katy: *you better not be late*
   Emily: *taking care of something. it's an emergency*
   Katy: *always is *eye roll**

Three months later...
Katy stood in front of the full-length mirror as Emily adjusted her wedding veil, secured by her crown, one more time. Her dress, a ball gown fit for dragon royalty, was custom-made by the finest designers, the huge black diamond pendant and earrings Ryker had given her secure about her neck and ears. All she was missing was her ring, and that would be placed on her finger within the hour. "Are you sure you're all right with this, Em?"

Emily gave her a gentle squeeze, careful not to mess up either of their dresses or makeup. "I've told you a hundred times, you and Ryker are meant to be together, but you just won't let it go, so now I feel like I have to confess something to you or this is going to haunt us both forever. Sit, dear Sister; this might take a moment."

Katy sank onto the edge of the chair and looked at her twin. Her sister wore a dress nearly identical to her own, only slightly less massive, and black. As in, dragon-made black. Emily knew everything now. Her mother, too. Katy had insisted. She couldn't live a lie. Never again. "What is it, Em?"

Emily glanced at their mother, who rested comfortably on the sofa, her gentle snore reassuring both girls. She was still recovering from the fire, but thanks to Draquonir influence and wealth, she was receiving the very best treatments.

"Emily! Spill it!" Katy couldn't take the suspense. Her sister was always so dramatic. If she had something to say about her and Ryker, she needed to say it now, before it was too late. Her heart pounded in fear.

Emily took a deep breath and let it out. "Okay. Here goes. You know how when I called you and said I needed your help, you told me 'no more breaking up with my boyfriends'?"

Katy's eyes narrowed suspiciously. "Yes?"

"Well, I had already decided not to go through with the whole thing, but I spent the advance on Mom's hospital bills..."

Katy didn't think she could get any more tense, her whole body on edge, but she was wrong. "Go on."

Emily adjusted her dress, smoothed and rearranged the heavy train. "I had put them off three times already. They refused to wait any more. And I figured since he wasn't really my boyfriend, you wouldn't really be breaking up for me."

Katy fumed. She knew Emily sometimes had a strange way of making things work out exactly the way she wanted, but none of what she said was making any sense to her. "If you wanted out, then why did you insist I go over there and sign the damn contract?"

"I told you," Emily huffed, "I already spent the advance. The only way I wouldn't have to pay it back was if they cancelled the contract. I figured all I had to do was send you in my place to sign the contract, and then you would be you and everything would work out."

Katy slowly rose from the chair, her hand clenched around a small ivory pillow. She took a menacing step toward Emily, her emotions equal parts rage and joy. She took another step closer to her target. Emily was going to pay this time. "Let me get this straight, Twin: you sent me to your fiancé hoping I would screw things up and he would break up with me? I mean, you?"

"Yeees? Sorry about that."

That was the last straw. Katy smacked her sister with the pillow. Once. Twice. "Evil! You brat!"

Emily screamed. Laughed. Grabbed the pillow and

a tug-of-war ensued. "Katy! You can't be mad at me. Look how it turned out! I was right! You messed everything up, he cancelled the contract, and you got a billionaire dragon husband who is not only completely in love with you, he made you immortal!"

Emily screamed again as Katy got control of the pillow and hit her again, her eyes flashing with dragonfire.

Ryker, Vector, and Fury barreled through the door like the house was on fire, roaring a battle cry, searching for the source of danger.

Katy and Emily froze, mid-fight, at the spectacle. Their mother, asleep until then, sat up gingerly and yawned. "Is it time?"

Ryker was the first to recover. He straightened from his defensive stance and adjusted his necktie. "We heard screaming."

Katy stared at Ryker, her heart on her sleeve as she watched him fidget nervously. "Everything is fine, mate."

He came over and kissed her tenderly. She dropped the pillow to wrap her arms around him, her anger with her sister gone as quickly as it had arisen. Today was not the day for anger. Today was about her and Ryker and spending the rest of their lives together.

Ryker cleared his throat, his eyes soft. Full of love. "We are ready for you, *Mia Regina*. Do you not hear the dragon song?"

Katy cocked her head, listening. A deep, guttural

rhythm soaked into her being, some of the notes so low she could feel them in her chest but couldn't hear them, while others rang out in a perfect harmony. "It's beautiful. What is it?"

"The unmated dragons, both male and female, sing our family song. It is traditional. They sing our ancient Draquonir lineage. They sing of hope. Our future. They sing of finding their own true mates. They sing of us."

Katy blinked away tears, happy tears. "Go ahead then. We'll be right down."

Ryker kissed her once more, their fingertips clinging together, both reluctant to end the connection.

Katy watched Ryker and his Guardians walk out and quietly close the door behind them. Emily, who'd been silent until now, whistled softly.

"Damn, girl. He's got it bad."

"He's a hunk." Their mother offered from the sofa.

Katy and Emily turned in shock to stare at their mother with identical slack jaws and open mouths. Their mother did not talk about men. Not since their father had passed.

"Mom!" Emily's exclamation was followed by giggling.

Their mother rose to her feet and held out her hands, one to each of her beautiful, precious daughters. "Come along, you two. We don't want Katy's hunk to get away."

They walked together, the twins each holding one of their mother's arms, both as an act of solidarity and to make sure she didn't lose her balance.

When they reached the entrance to the courtyard, two large Guardians waited to open the double doors, each dressed in shimmering clan black.

Their mother sighed. "If I was thirty years younger, you boys would be in trouble."

A grin from one of the men was the only response as Katy and Emily surrounded their mother in one final group hug.

"Let's do this," Emily said.

"I love you girls. I'm so proud of you. So happy." She started to cry, and Katy shushed her.

"Mom, don't you dare do that. I'll start crying too and ruin my makeup!"

"Go on then. Go."

With one final squeeze for the women she loved, the women who had supported her, loved her, and made her who she was, Katy turned to face the doors and nodded to the Guardian. "I'm ready."

"Very good, *Mia Regina*."

That title coming from lips other than Ryker's was going to take some getting used to.

The doors opened, and she was enveloped in sound, the dragon song a chorus of voices more beautiful than a Mendelssohn choir, the song, far older. She could feel the ancient weight of the chorus as the melodies flowed over and around one another, each dragon lifting a unique voice to the skies to offer thanks for their new queen, their new hope for a brighter future.

As their tradition required, Katy walked down the center of the aisle with her family walking behind her in a show of support for the union. Coming from the opposite direction, Ryker walked with Vector just behind. And behind Vector? Dozens of Draquonir in stunning black gowns and suits, some in ceremonial armor carrying sparkling swords, others in modern suits or gowns with glittering black diamonds on their cuff links, their earrings, bracelets. Everywhere she looked, Katy sensed dragonfire. Magic.

The effect was startling. Ethereal. She felt like a fairy princess in a magical story with the fairy-tale prince waiting for her in the center of the courtyard.

Their people, their combined families surrounded the couple in a circle, all parts supporting the new family, the new beginning at their center.

Ryker held out his hand to Katy, and she placed her palm in his. He slipped the ring she'd chosen onto her finger. "Keeper of my heart. True mate. I am eternally yours."

Around them the song rose to a crescendo, the magic of dragonfire building in Katy's chest as the dragon within Ryker poured his own vow into her once more. Protection. Honor. Immortality. Love.

The dragonfire engulfed her from head to toe. Her slippers. Her gown. Her flesh. But it did not burn.

Across from her, Ryker shifted, his dragon towering over her small frame in the courtyard, the dragon doing its best to look regal. Perfect. Katy could sense his need for her acceptance in front of the others. Even dragons needed their mate to love them, accept them.

"Ryker. Dragon. Keepers of my heart," Katy began, "I am your true mate as you are mine. I am eternally yours."

The circle opened just enough for one man to walk forward. Katy recognized him as the dark elf. He was a prince and one of Ryker's oldest friends.

He'd also come to the estate to shove his black sword straight into Ryker's heart. Katy hadn't quite forgiven him for that.

Sparkles and flashes of light surrounded them. The circle disappeared in a magical fog. When it cleared, the elf, Katy, and her mother and sister were the only creatures left who didn't have scales.

They were surrounded by a circle of dragons. Huge. Fierce. A terror for any enemy. A powerful clan bound by ties of blood and honor.

Ryker lifted his head to the sky and roared.

As one, the others lifted their heads and joined him, the sound unlike anything Katy had ever heard before.

"Katherine Toure, I am Prince Alrik, protector and executioner of this dragon clan. Do you accept this dragon as your mate? Do you accept his dragonfire and his children? Do you vow to protect the knowledge of our existence from all who would threaten us?"

Katy stared up into the jeweled eyes of the black dragon, the beautiful beast she knew as her love in another form. "Yes. I do."

In a flash Ryker stood before her, not as a dragon but as a man. Her man. Her mate. The love of her life.

She held out her hand this time. Ryker took it, and the elf, Prince Alrik, wrapped their hands together with a golden chain Katy recognized as the one Ryker used to wear around his neck. She knew what those chains meant now. Knew that nearly every dragon in this clan was forced to wear them. That her union with Ryker was the first in hundreds of years. That before this day, the Draquonir had nearly given up hope. For many, the executioner's blade was the final and only honorable choice left to them.

Silence descended on the courtyard, and Prince Alrik spoke.

"I bind you with dragon chains. I bind you with dragonfire. I bind you with love."

Ryker could not tear his eyes from his bride. He stepped forward and pulled her into his arms, kissed her with every ounce of love and reverence he had in his heart.

Katy's dragonfire erupted to surround them in heat and desire and love, the black flames dancing around and between them as within, his dragon howled with contentment and the dragons around them roared their approval of the union.

Katy was now a queen. A member of the Draquonir. Ryker's one true mate.

Forever.

A SPECIAL THANK YOU TO MY READERS...

Want more? I've got **hidden** bonus content on my web site *exclusively* for those on my <u>mailing list</u>.

If you are already on my email list, you don't need to do a thing! Simply scroll to the bottom of my newsletter emails and click on the **super-secret** link.

Not a member? What are you waiting for? In addition to ALL of my bonus content (great new stuff will be added regularly) you will be the first to hear about my newest release the second it hits the stores—AND you will get a free book as a special welcome gift.

Sign up now! http://freescifiromance.com

FIND YOUR INTERSTELLAR MATCH!

YOUR mate is out there. Take the test today and discover your perfect match. Are you ready for a sexy alien mate (or two)?

VOLUNTEER NOW!

interstellarbridesprogram.com

DO YOU LOVE AUDIOBOOKS?

Grace Goodwin's books are now available as
audiobooks...everywhere.

LET'S TALK!

Interested in joining my **Sci-Fi Squad**? Meet new like-minded sci-fi romance fanatics and chat with Grace! Get excerpts, cover reveals and sneak peeks before anyone else. Be part of a private Facebook group that shares pictures and fun news! Join here:

https://www.facebook.com/groups/scifisquad/

Want to talk about Grace Goodwin books with others? Join the **SPOILER ROOM** and spoil away! Your GG BFFs are waiting! (And so is Grace) Join here:

https://www.facebook.com/groups/ggspoilerroom/

GET A FREE BOOK!

ALSO BY GRACE GOODWIN

Starfighter Training Academy

The First Starfighter

Starfighter Command

Elite Starfighter

Interstellar Brides® Program: The Beasts

Bachelor Beast

Maid for the Beast

Beauty and the Beast

The Beasts Boxed Set

Interstellar Brides® Program

Assigned a Mate

Mated to the Warriors

Claimed by Her Mates

Taken by Her Mates

Mated to the Beast

Mastered by Her Mates

Tamed by the Beast

Mated to the Vikens

Her Mate's Secret Baby

Mating Fever

Her Viken Mates

Fighting For Their Mate

Her Rogue Mates

Claimed By The Vikens

The Commanders' Mate

Matched and Mated

Hunted

Viken Command

The Rebel and the Rogue

Rebel Mate

Surprise Mates

Interstellar Brides® Program Boxed Set - Books 6-8

Interstellar Brides® Program Boxed Set - Books 9-12

Interstellar Brides® Program Boxed Set - Books 13-16

Interstellar Brides® Program Boxed Set - Books 17-20

Interstellar Brides® Program: The Colony

Surrender to the Cyborgs

Mated to the Cyborgs

Cyborg Seduction

Her Cyborg Beast

Cyborg Fever

Rogue Cyborg

Cyborg's Secret Baby

Her Cyborg Warriors

Claimed by the Cyborgs

The Colony Boxed Set 1

The Colony Boxed Set 2

Interstellar Brides® Program: The Virgins

The Alien's Mate

His Virgin Mate

Claiming His Virgin

His Virgin Bride

His Virgin Princess

The Virgins - Complete Boxed Set

Interstellar Brides® Program: Ascension Saga

Ascension Saga, book 1

Ascension Saga, book 2

Ascension Saga, book 3

Trinity: Ascension Saga - Volume 1

Ascension Saga, book 4

Ascension Saga, book 5

Ascension Saga, book 6

Faith: Ascension Saga - Volume 2

Ascension Saga, book 7

Ascension Saga, book 8

Ascension Saga, book 9

Destiny: Ascension Saga - Volume 3

Other Books

Their Conquered Bride

Wild Wolf Claiming: A Howl's Romance

Dragon Chains

ALSO BY BECCA BRAYDEN

LUMERIAN KNIGHTS

Alien King Crashes the Wedding

Alien Knight Steals the Bride

Alien Knight Blind Date Disaster

Alien Knight Teddy Bear Troubles

Now available in AUDIO!

ABOUT GRACE

Grace Goodwin is a USA Today and international best-selling author of Sci-Fi and Paranormal romance with more than one million books sold. Grace's titles are available worldwide in multiple languages in ebook, print and audio formats.

Grace loves to hear from readers! All of Grace's books can be read as sexy, stand-alone adventures. But be careful, she likes her heroes hot and her love scenes hotter. You have been warned...

www.gracegoodwin.com
gracegoodwinauthor@gmail.com

ABOUT BECCA

Becca Brayden spends her days writing and her nights dreaming up her next hot adventure with even hotter alien hunks. A Colorado native, she has lived in New Zealand, Florida, Alabama, Kansas and loves to travel in direct proportion to how much she hates to cook. Chocolate makes her happy, licorice makes her cringe, and despite the cult following - she hates pumpkin pie and pumpkin spice lattes. (More for you!)

Natural wanderlust has given her a deep love for Mediterranean food and a bookshelf filled with everything from philosophy to sexy romance and hard core sci-fi. You can catch her enjoying a cup of hot cocoa on her Facebook page. facebook.com/authorbecca-brayden